Some Kind of Love

ELLE WRIGHT

Elle Wrights Books, LLC
Ypsilanti, Michigan
www.ElleWright.com

Copy Editor/Proofreading:
Paulette Nunlee
5-Star Proofing

Cover Design:
Sherelle Green

Some Kind of Love

TAYLAR

I'm a professional. I have strict rules of conduct when it comes to my business, Taylar Made Events.

My number one rule? Don't flirt with the groom.

But… What about the groom's moody, but *hot* brother?

KEON

When I agreed to pay for my brother's wedding, I didn't know he was marrying the Wicked Witch of the East. I also didn't realize I'd find myself fantasizing about the wedding planner.

The Problem? She's my best friend's little sister. The curve of her hips and the fullness of her lips are none of my business.

Now… I just have to remember that.

Dear Reader

It's been a tough several months!

I can't thank you all enough for rocking with me. I truly appreciate your support as I took an extended break from writing.

I couldn't help but fall in love with Taylar when she helped her brother Maddox win Sloane's heart. I loved her ability to speak her mind. Can you tell I love all my heroines like this? LOL

Anyway, creating this story was the palate cleanser I needed. I enjoyed this close-knit group of friend and family. "*Framily*" as I call it. And Keon... Lawd. Talk about the strong, silent type. This man has been through it!!! And Taylor is the woman waiting for him at the end of his journey to happiness.

I hope you enjoy Keon and Taylar as much as I did!

Love,

Elle

<u>www.ellewright.com</u>

Recommended Reading

Some Kind of Love is the start of a standalone series featuring the men who own Smoke and Burn Cigar Lounge. Taylar is the younger sister of Maddox Cross, who found his *Happily Ever After* with one of my fave heroines in TEN CHRISTMAS SHOTS. If you'd like to get acquainted with this family before you read, I recommend starting with that story.

There are two things I've always hated about December: Yuletide and Carols.

Apparently, my besties are tired of my Scrooge-like behavior. Instead of commiserating with me at my annual *non*Christmas, *forever*Single party, they're forcing me to go on a luxury trip to the worst *magical* place on Earth—for two.

I've never been girlfriend material. Too much work, not enough good feelings. Now I have ten dates, ten shots to find a plus one. The one caveat? My friends pick the dates—even ex-boyfriends are not off limits.

Dealing with the past, stepping outside of my comfort zone, meeting strangers… What can go wrong? Everything. Or nothing. I can't decide which is scarier. A long time ago, I vowed to only let my brain make the important decisions. What if my heart didn't get the memo?

For Jerry, thanks for being my friend. You are so missed.

Prologue

MY BAT-SHIT CRAZY LIFE

TAYLAR

Part I

Too Hot

Several Years Ago

"**F**uck you and that bitch you brought home last night!"

It's not that hard. Really. *And I'm smart, dammit.* Except when I confused *good* dick with *good* guy. Somehow, I'd failed that test time and again. At this point in my life, I should've learned my lesson. I didn't consider myself a true playa, and trust me… I knew several women who got theirs and kept it moving. More power to them. That just wasn't me. Aside from a single one-night stand in college, I preferred sex within the safe confines of a monogamous relationship. Yet, I couldn't even count the number of times I'd been betrayed by a beautiful dark chocolate dick attached to a fine-as-hell weird-ass, stupid-ass, jealous-ass muthafucka with baggage. This time, though, I was caught up in a love spat between my "man" and the woman who had a key to his house and called herself his girlfriend.

The woman banged on the bedroom door. "Come out, Bitch!"

This can't be my life. My family had always teased me about my taste in men. My father called me a bum magnet. Based on my last several boyfriends, my dad might've been on to something. I blamed him, though. It was his impossible standards that made me want to rebel. From the blind dates with his colleagues to the constant complaining about my singlehood, it was no wonder I was attracted to men who were the total opposite of what I knew my parents wanted for me. But Hector was different… or so I'd thought.

When we'd met at a fundraiser, Hector had impressed me. Mostly because he could speak to anything. Politics, sports, books, movies, food… He was an entrepreneur, a business owner who'd turned one real estate investment into several vacation rentals. During dinner last night, he reiterated his commitment to making me happy, to showing me he was serious about me. Which was why I'd gone against my own rules and went to his place. *Damn.* I couldn't believe the turn of events.

"Can you chill out, Chandra?" Hector grumbled. After ten minutes of her screaming at the top of her lungs about betrayal, broken engagements, and countless lies, this nigga finally spoke up. "What the hell are you doing here? I'm single."

Another loud knock or five later, Chandra shouted, "When I see her, I'm fucking her up!"

My head hurts. I considered climbing out of the window, until I glanced at my reflection in the mirror. The batshit crazy girl still spewing threats was right. All my shit was in the living room. With them. My lack of clothing and hangover was no match for her level of rage.

In my haste to get fucked, I'd left my keys, my dress, my purse, my shoes, and my common sense out there. I didn't even want to think about the lecture my mother would give me if she could see me now. Top of the list of things *not* to do is leave your purse in another room while you're sleeping. The sex had been amazing, though, starting from the moment he took me against his front door and ending with his tongue on my clit early this morning. *Damn*, my underwear was out there too? And my bra. And my phone. *Shit, Taylar, you fucked up.*

The only thing I had with me was my… I hurried to the bedside table and picked up my Apple Watch. Luckily, the battery hadn't died. I whispered a text to my brother who had my location: *Come get me. Now.*

A loud scream and the sound of broken glass on the other side of the door forced me to look for a weapon to protect myself, because… Shit, I had no idea what I'd find when I left the room. I searched his drawers, looking for something other than his t-shirt to wear. I found an oversized shirt and a pair of sweatpants, and quickly slipped them on. Climbing on top of the dresser, I flung open the blinds and bit out a low curse when I noticed the bars on the window.

The argument outside the bedroom was in full swing. As both of them hurled insults at each other, I practiced a karate kick and a weak-ass uppercut to the air. Only to fall back on the bed. Staring at the ceiling, I whispered to whoever I thought could hear me beyond the physical realm, "Granny, you once told me never to trust someone with shifty eyes, and I didn't listen. But he's so fine. And you told me to never drink that nasty-ass gin, but it's part of the Long Island so I did. It was good, though. Okay, God, I would tell you that I wouldn't have premarital sex, but you already know I'm a work in progress. I learned my lesson, though. Maybe. Please let me get out of this without having to fight. `Cause y'all know I haven't lifted a fist since Hailey Palmer pulled my ponytail out during homeroom class in ninth grade. I'm not cut out for this. Amen. Oh, and—"

"Chandra, stop!" Hector roared, after the dog whimpered.

Did she kick the dog? I picked up the nearest weapon.

"That's my dog too," Chandra blared over the puppy's piercing bark. "I'm taking him with me!"

What the hell are they doing out there? I checked my watch. Ryker hadn't responded yet, but that didn't mean he didn't see the text. If anything, my big brother was already on his way to save the day.

The doorbell chimed, and I sent up a silent prayer of thanks. But the voice that pierced the silence wasn't Ryker. Wait a minute... "It's the police," I murmured to myself. My shoulders sagged as relief washed over me. Not only did I not have to fight, but I didn't have to use my handy dandy weapon either. I set the lamp down and tiptoed toward the door.

I listened as the cop assessed the situation, and then I took a chance and cracked the door open. All eyes landed on me, and I waved. "Hi."

I scanned the living room. Pillows were strewn on the floor, the dog was eating food that had spattered on the rug. Glass was shattered on the furniture and one of the officers was handcuffing the woman who continued to spew threats at me as I emerged from the bedroom.

I met Hector's gaze with a hard glare and fought the urge to slap the shit out of him for putting me in that situation. "Where's my stuff?"

"I ripped that shit up," Chandra taunted.

"Shut the hell up, Chandra," Hector growled. He handed me what was left of my dress. "I'm sorry. Can you stay? I'll make breakfast."

I raised a questioning brow. "You can't be serious."

Hector approached me tentatively. "I am. It's complicated."

"Obviously."

"Is that your Lexus SUV outside, miss?" an officer asked.

I nodded. "Yes. What's wrong?"

"Ms. Payne admitted to vandalizing the vehicle," he explained. "I'm happy to call a tow company for you."

"I can't drive it?"

The officer flashed a sad smile. "Not at this time. Not with four flat tires."

I murmured a curse. "Thanks, Officer. I'll take care of it."

Officer Kennedy led me over to the kitchen. After he took my statement, he gave me his card. "Thanks, Miss Cross. Can I drop you anywhere?"

I gathered the rest of my things. "That would be great."

A soft knock echoed in the quiet house. "What's up?" Hector asked, a hard edge to his voice.

"I'm here for her."

I recognized the voice immediately, and it wasn't my brother Ryker. It wasn't my other brother, Maddox either. I blinked. "Keon?"

Intense, dark eyes bore into me, raked over me, almost like he was checking every inch of my body to be sure I was okay. "You good?"

"Ryker sent you?"

"Are you good, Taylar?" he repeated, never breaking eye contact with me.

I swallowed. Growing up, my brother's friends had always treated me like their little sister. They got on my nerves, scared away every boy in school, and raided my stash of junk food all the time, but they'd always protected me. Even now, I could count on them to step in when Ryker couldn't.

My fourteen-year-old self would have sworn Keon secretly wanted me to be his soulmate for life. It was the way he looked at me that always made me question everything I thought I knew. Of course, he'd never done or said anything inappropriate. He'd never been anything but a perfect gentleman, even though I'd imagined whispered declarations of secret love, stolen glances, and steamy makeout sessions behind my brother's back.

"Taylar?" Keon called again.

"I'm okay," I croaked. "I'm fine. Thanks for coming."

"Can we talk?" Hector asked. "I—"

I brushed past him. "I have nothing to say to you."

Hector reached out to grab me, but I maneuvered away from his grasp. "Taylar, listen."

"You heard what she said." Keon glared at Hector. "Lose her number. You don't want those problems."

As I neared Keon, I realized I felt lighter, like I could breathe again. I felt safe. "I'm ready."

Keon searched my eyes, took my hand, and led me out of the house. The car ride back home was eerily silent. No doubt, I was grateful that he came. But the embarrassment I felt had eclipsed the gratitude.

I swallowed past a lump in my throat. "Please don't tell anyone about this." Tears welled up in my eyes. "I don't want my dad to find out."

Election day was right around the corner. The last thing my father needed was a scandal to prevent him from winning his heavily-favored race to become a member of the Michigan House of Representatives. The campaign had worked hard to get him to this point, and I hated the thought of being the reason he wouldn't be able to succeed.

"You know that's not who I am, Taylar." Everyone else called me Tay or sis, but Keon had never used a nickname to refer to me.

"Not even Ryker?"

He smirked. "Not even Ryker," he agreed.

I sunk into the leather seat of his truck. "Thanks. And... don't mention it. I mean, this. Ever again."

"Your secret is safe with me."

&

Part II

Too Cold

December, Year Before Last

I'D WAITED all day for this orgasm—during the early breakfast at Cracker Barrel, through the nasty-ass lunch his mother had prepared, and while he schmoozed his boss during their annual Holiday party. Canceling my plans with my bestie and rescheduling pedicures with Mom seemed like a fair trade for the promise of good sex.

Deion pinned me against the bedroom door, wrapped his hand around my neck and kissed me. Never mind he tasted like beef and garlic, I just wanted to feel something other than what I'd been feeling for the past several days. Misunderstood. Neglected. *Alone.*

We stumbled through my condo toward the bedroom. Always the bedroom. Always on the bed. Always missionary. Always the same. But I didn't care. I needed this. My boyfriend lowered me on the mattress. He smiled at me and brushed his lips over mine.

"Love you," he murmured.

The two words hung in the air. He'd been saying it since we met last year after the first time we had sex. Hell, he'd said it every day after that. And I'd never said it back.

Instead of replying with a "love you" or even "you too," I

kissed him. I just couldn't bring myself to utter the words. Because... *I don't love him*.

Deion was the oldest son of Dwight Alexander, former NBA player and current owner of a soul food restaurant chain serving Detroit and its surrounding areas. Unlike his father, Deion wasn't a star baller, hated soul food, and preferred the quiet life away from the spotlight. We'd met when he was hired as the VP of Analytics & Insights at my former place of employment where I worked as a Human Resources manager. From the beginning, he'd been a gentleman only asking me out once he was sure it wasn't against company policy. After the debacle with Hector, though, I wasn't sure I wanted to get involved again. I turned him down that day. But we became work friends, then real friends. Soon, we were spending hours just talking or hanging out. The decision to segue from friendship to romance had been easy because I genuinely liked him as a person. I felt safe with him. The only problem? He—

"Do you want me?" he murmured.

I glanced up at the ceiling, unsure how to respond to that since we were already naked, and his not-that-impressive-but-alright dick was mere inches away from my pussy. I went with the obvious answer. "Of course."

Without another word, he thrust forward and all talking ceased. Yet, before I could get my rhythm, before I could get my orgasm, Deion's patented growl assured that my hopes were about to be dashed. Then, he came.

And *that* was the problem. Sex. I'd traded unforgettable fucks anywhere I wanted for two-minute missionary dick. No matter what I did to get him—and myself—in the mood, how I psyched myself out to be with him, when we did it... It simply sucked.

Frustrated, I pushed his ass off me and stomped into the bathroom. After a long shower with my toy dick, I felt a little less irritated when I emerged, only to find him sprawled out and snoring loudly on *my* damn bed. Shaking my head, I pulled my favorite blanket off the bed, grabbed my phone, and made my way to my office.

Work would always be there, even if the dick wasn't, so I got to it. I made the decision to leave my corporate job and start my own business, Taylar Made Events. It had started as a part-time side hustle and had morphed into my destiny. Despite the demands of being my own boss, crazy bridezillas, crying babies and their mamas, prickly future mothers-in-law, unattached but rich fathers of the bride, long days, and unpredictable nights, I loved it.

Several emails, a design board, and two wedding timeline drafts later, I rested my head against the chair. My phone buzzed across my desk and I glanced over at the clock. It was nearly midnight, so the text could only be from one person. I snickered when I read the message from my best friend.

KiKi: *Girl, go to sleep.*

I peeked out of my office window and waved at my bestie, who was standing on her balcony holding a glass of wine. Living in the same development as my friend had its benefits. She always had food, wine, and an open door. Any hope of hiding anything from her, though, had vanished the moment I turned on my light. Instead of texting her back, I called her.

"What are you doing up?" I asked. "It's way past wine o'clock."

"I could ask you the same question. Aren't you supposed to be getting some right now, Tay?"

There wasn't much my bestie didn't know about me. Twenty-five years of friendship made every subject game for conversation. Even my non-existent sex life. "The good news is I got my orgasm," I murmured, switching to video chat.

I smiled when Akira appeared on my screen, wearing her oversized bonnet and a wide grin that faded when her gaze swept over my face. "Seriously? Your hair isn't even messed up."

"It's over," I shrugged, "but I came."

She arched a brow. "*He* made you come? Or did you have to take matters into your own hands?"

I eyed the open door. At any moment, Deion could pop into the room, and then I'd have to explain this conversation. Which would then morph into another discussion about telling my friend about our private life. "Shhh. He's sleep."

"Should I take that as your answer?" She shrugged. "Hey. Good thing you just ordered a new B.A.D. last week."

"That is a bright side," I agreed. The Big Ass D was my fave toy dick. I'd already gone through three of those things since I got with Deion, which was a damn shame. I had a real dick in the other room, and it didn't work right. But the B.A.D. was always clutch in crucial horny situations.

She sighed. "Tay, it's time to let it go. You've given this relationship your all. I don't think I've ever seen you this sad and unhappy."

And unfulfilled. And bored. "I'm not sad. I'm just tired. I have so much to do to prepare for next weekend." Due to the nature of my job, my weekends were pretty much reserved for clients. And next weekend, I had a wedding and my very first Mistletoe Match. I'd partnered with a friend to help match people with their forever baes. "Can I still count on your help to decorate the bar?"

"Of course," she said. "I'll be there early to help hang all the mistletoe. But back to you…"

"I changed the subject for a reason, Kira. I don't want to talk about it. Deion is a good guy," I argued. "I can depend on him to pay his bills and to come home at night."

"But you can't depend on him to fuck the shit out of you. I'm sure there are men that can pay bills, come home, and not suck in bed." When I didn't respond right away, she continued, "In your heart, you know he's not right for you."

Every day, I made up a different excuse to stay with him.

One of the biggest reasons keeping me there was it was easy. Being with Deion came with one very priceless benefit. He was drama-free. I didn't have to worry about side chicks, secret baby mamas coming out of the woodwork, or police knocking on the door to execute a search warrant. And my father loved him, which was no small feat considering Michigan State Representative Ryan Cross had never liked anyone I dated.

"A crazy office breakup is off the table because you don't work with him anymore," Kira mused. "Whispers from colleagues about you? Fuck them messy heffas anyway. Your father just doesn't want you to date any more criminals or freeloaders or men with fucked-up girlfriends. But most importantly, Deion is not blessing you with good dick. So what is it?"

"I told you… He's successful, he treats me with respect, and we have fun together."

Kira frowned. "When do you have fun? At his parents' house when you have to sit through those Saturday brunches? While he's doing his logic puzzles before he falls asleep?"

"I like Sudoku," I lied. "We do them together."

She scoffed. "Yeah right. You hate that shit. Just like you hate his garlic breath and his parents. You—"

"Enough," I whisper-yelled, checking the hallway again. "I don't want him to hear you."

"Would it be so bad if he did?" she challenged. "Maybe he would do something different than what he's been doing since you got with him?"

"And you've just proven Deion's point."

"What does that even mean? What point?"

"He told me I talk too much. And it's pretty obvious *who* I need to stop talking to."

Cracking up, Kira waved a dismissive hand. "That's fair. I'll shut up."

"I should probably get off the phone. He might come looking for me."

"Do you even believe that?"

No.

"You've always told me to follow my heart," she said.

"And you've yet to tell my brother how you feel about him." My best friend had set her sights on my oldest brother, Broderick, when we were in elementary school. Despite my many warnings, she'd placed him on a pedestal he didn't belong on. As a result, she'd set herself up for heartbreak because my brother was the worst kind of man. Unfaithful, unreliable, and unworthy. "When you tell my brother how you feel, come talk to me."

"I have a plan," she insisted. "I'll do it on my timeline."

"Whatever you say."

"So maybe we're both full of shit?"

I giggled. "I love you, Kira."

"Love you too. Get some sleep. Maybe Mr. Unsexy will wake you up for middle of the night sex."

The thought of him touching me was enough to convince me to turn on a movie and fall asleep on the couch tonight. But instead of telling my friend that, I simply said, "Hopefully."

We made plans to meet for lunch tomorrow before I hung up. I took my time straightening up my space.

"Baby?" Deion called from the doorway.

"Hey." I forced a smile. "I was just finishing up in here."

He held out his hand and waited for me to take it. Pulling me to him, he brushed his lips over my forehead. "Come to bed."

I wanted to tell him to go to hell, but I couldn't. In the grand scheme of my life, Deion was better than most of the men I've dated. I liked him. And most of my family liked him too.

"Babe?" His soft voice pulled me out of my thoughts. "Are you okay?"

I met his waiting gaze and nodded. "Sure."

"Come on."

As I let him lead me to the bedroom for a night of cuddling, I wondered... *Is that enough*?

CHAPTER 1

Mary Go Round

TAYLAR

February, This Year

Willpower is overrated. Which is why I murmured, "Fuck it" and bit into the Snickers bar hidden beneath the bag of celery and the Greek yogurt in the small refrigerator under my desk. Unfortunately for me, the woman crying hadn't even realized that I'd zoned out.

While my controlling and far-too-condescending client wailed about her stupid bridesmaids and their dress woes, the flowers, her matron of honor's pregnancy, her mother's growing guest list, and her fiancé's lack of support, I savored the chocolate and caramel... and nuts. *The only satisfying nuts I've seen in months.*

I took another slow bite of my candy bar and made a mental note to buy more—for the Valentine's party, of course.

After all, I hadn't bought this one. It was a leftover gift from my Christmas stocking. *Thank God for Mom*.

The sound of a throat clearing brought me back to the present. Glancing over, I offered the soon-to-be-groom a sad smile. Rashaad Webb had finally met the woman he wanted to make his wife, and she was an ungrateful, spiteful, entitled bitch. And, yes, I'd told him that on more than one occasion. But since, he was my brother's friend, I'd relented and agreed to plan their hurried nuptials.

While his future bride, Meri, droned on about everything except for the rehearsal dinner—which was the purpose of this meeting—he mouthed, "Be nice."

When Meri finally stopped talking, I met her gaze. "Didn't the designer lower the hem of the dresses to hide their shoes?" I asked.

"Yes, but—"

"Problem solved. No one will see the ankle tattoos and bracelets." She opened her mouth to speak but I rushed on. "Did you check your email?"

Did I forget to mention that I knew Meri? Meri Donovan was the daughter of my father's lawyer. While I'd known her practically my entire life, I never liked her. My resentment started from the moment my parents made me play hopscotch with her when I wanted to play ball with my brothers. Planning her wedding had been a nightmare from the very beginning, but Rashaad had begged me to help them. Oh, and my father bribed me with a vacation.

She frowned, lifting her phone. "I wasn't aware that you'd sent me anything."

I forced a smile. "Your big day is right around the corner. I really need you to review the final timeline and send me any changes."

"Okay, but the flowers—"

"After our last meeting, I contacted the florist about your concerns. Since you don't want the wedding to be 'too corny',

I thought it would be nice to incorporate Casablanca Lilies or even orchids into your arrangements. Even with the tight deadline, she was able to order the flowers. I forwarded pictures to your email."

Meri stared at her phone. "I love it," she whispered. "Thank you."

I rested my elbows on my desk and leaned forward. "I'll have staff on site that will step in to handle unruly guests. No need to worry about that. As for your sister, she's carrying your nephew." I shrugged. "You can't change that. The only thing you can do is kick her out of the wedding, but is it worth hurting her feelings and potentially ruining your relationship with her because she has a baby bump?"

"You're right." Meri glanced over at Rashaad and murmured, "I can't tell if she's making fun of me."

"I'm not," I assured her. "I can't stress enough that your marriage is more important than this wedding."

"You don't have to tell me that," Meri argued. "I know. But this wedding is important too. I want everything to be beautiful."

"Great!" I chirped. "We're on the same page, then. I understand all of your concerns and I'm here to help. I would also encourage you to sit down with your mother and have a conversation. It can't hurt to voice your concerns about the growing guest list as well as her unexpected and unannounced visits to your home."

Meri gasped and smacked Rashaad on his shoulder. "You told her?"

Yikes. I slid down in my chair. The other day, I'd overheard Ryker and Rashaad talking about an interrupted blow job. "My bad," I grumbled.

Rashaad glared at me, then looked at his fiancée with soft eyes. "Calm down, baby. It's not what you think."

As Meri whisper-yelled at Rashaad about keeping their business in their house, I looked down at my phone. Ten missed calls and many more texts. Frowning, I unlocked my phone and browsed my call log. Six of the calls were from Deion and the rest were from every member of my family except my oldest brother, Broderick. Most of the texts were from Deion and my family as well, with a few from Kira and one from Keon. My stomach dropped because my family didn't text or call like this unless something was wrong. And since I needed to stay focused on the matter at hand, I chose to open the message from Keon first.

Keon: *Are you still with Rashaad?*

I loved that Keon never wasted words on bullshit. He was straight, to the point in everything he did. I glanced up at the *happy* couple. Well, Rashaad looked downright miserable as Meri continued to point out his flaws. For the first time ever, I wanted to smack the shit out of a client. And it wasn't the bride. It was the man she was marrying—the man who'd just let her blame him for everything wrong with their wedding, even her sister's pregnancy. The man who was on the verge of ruining his life by exchanging vows with that twit. That same man had single handedly stomped the shit out of a gang leader who'd threatened my brother's life back in high school. That same guy had nursed me back to health when I'd snuck into my father's cognac and passed out in front of his dorm room. The same asshole who never let me finish a sandwich if he was around. I loved that fool and I hated to see him go out like this.

Shaking my head, I typed out my response to Keon: *Yep. And he's getting nagged to death by your future sister-in-law.*

My phone rang then. Without a word, I stood and stepped out of my office. "Hey."

"Tell me again why this is a good idea."

The low tenor of his voice soothed something deep inside me as it always did. "It's not, but I've already shared my thoughts on the situation."

Keon didn't respond right away. I knew it had to be hard

on him watching his brother make the mistake of a lifetime. Especially since Keon had deemed himself Rashaad's protector when their parents died. Although they were only a year apart, Keon had worked his ass off to take care of his brother. Everything he made, he set aside some for Rashaad. Hell, he'd essentially paid for all of the groom's responsibilities including the rehearsal dinner and all the tuxedos for the groomsmen.

"Keon?" I called to him. "Are you there?"

He cleared his throat. "Send me the bill for the rehearsal dinner."

The sudden change in subject threw me off, but I rolled with it. "I told you it's on me." I'd already agreed to plan the rehearsal dinner at no additional charge as my gift to Rashaad. "Just make sure the bar is ready to be transformed."

"This is your business."

"He is my friend. More like my brother."

Another pause. Then… "I gotta go." The call ended signaling that he'd hung up on me.

If Keon was in front of me, I'd punch him because I hated when he did that. I also hated when he just walked away without saying goodbye. *Hate. It.*

So I fired off a text to him: *You suck.*

His lightning-fast response made me smile, though: *So.*

Before I walked back into my office, I opened the text chain from Deion and did a quick readthrough.

Deion: *Been trying to call you. Are we still on for dinner?*

Deion: *Is 6:00 still okay?*

Deion: *Call me!*

Deion: *Taylar, are you in meetings? What's going on? Call me!!*

Deion: *Are you still coming?!!!*

Deion: *It's not like you to avoid me. I need to know if we're still on!!!!*

Deion: *Love you. Call me!!!!!*

He'd sent a few more, all of them asking if I could still

make dinner tonight, all of them becoming increasingly frantic. I knew this because he added more exclamation points each time. The fact that he'd texted so much when I'd already told him I would be there gave me pause. Briefly, I thought about not going because my gut told me nothing good would come of it. But then… *Did I really want to have to explain myself later*? I blew out a harsh breath and sent him a quick text letting him know I'd be there. Again. Yet, even as I pressed SEND, I couldn't shake the feeling that something was off.

Back in my office, Rashaad was in his same seat, but Meri was all the way on the other side of the office with her arms folded and her back to him. "All set?" I asked.

Meri muttered a string of curses. "Is the rehearsal dinner all set?" she tossed back, with a hard roll of her eyes.

I met Rashaad's gaze with my patented you-better-get-your-girl glare. "Maybe you two should schedule a couple's massage. Think of it as a relationship-building exercise."

She waved a dismissive hand. "Did you become a wedding counselor in your off-season?"

I drummed my fingers against the table. "In less than a month, you'll be Mrs. Rashaad Webb."

"Right. And you'll still be *Ms.* Taylar Cross."

Rashaad stood then. "Don't talk to her like that."

Meri lifted her hands in exasperation. "Tell her to shut up and do the job we're paying her for, then. She's the reason we're arguing now!"

I opened my mouth to speak, but Rashaad shook his head. "Don't," he warned. He joined his future bride on the loveseat. "This is not Taylar's fault, baby."

"You're always protecting her." Meri's chin trembled before the tears came. "All of you. It's like she's your little princess or something."

"She's like my sister, and you know it." He kissed her brow. "Come on, baby. You know I love you."

Oh God. I wanted to throw up.

Meri's fake tears dried up and her permanent scowl was back. "It's *my* wedding. I'm not wrong for wanting *my* day to be a certain way."

"Then, we're good. I'll make sure *your* day happens the way you want it to." I pretended to jot down a note on a piece of paper. "I'll follow-up with the DJ tomorrow once you send me your overdue playlist." I stood. "I'm so excited about your big day!" Okay so I went a little overboard on my faux excitement, but I couldn't stop now. After all, this was my place of business. I couldn't really slap the bride. "It'll all be over soon."

I'd been around enough bitchy bridezillas to know when a couple was a lost cause. Not only was Meri a horrible person, but it was also obvious her marriage probably wouldn't last beyond their first anniversary—*if* they even made it to the altar.

It took a moment, but Meri finally stood. "I thought we were going to discuss the rehearsal? I'm still a little nervous about it. I hate that it's at a cigar bar."

"Not *a* cigar bar. It's your future *husband's* cigar bar," I pointed out. My brother Ryker, Keon, Rashaad, and their friend Antonio owned Smoke and Burn, a cigar lounge in downtown Ann Arbor. If she hadn't spent the entire hour complaining, maybe we could've had that discussion. "And everything is all set." Since this was my gift to him, I'd called in a favor with celebrity chef Duke Young and had spared no expense to transform the venue for the night.

"My father told me you didn't call his chef. What if I don't like the food?"

I counted to ten fast and prayed for patience. "You'll love it. The chef is amazing."

"He better be," she grumbled.

Ignoring her comment, I said, "If anything comes up, call me. I'm here to help."

Meri rolled her eyes. "Sometimes, it doesn't feel like it."

I sucked in another calming breath that didn't work. "Other than that, I'll see you at our final meeting." I smiled. "Rest assured, I have everything under control."

Rashaad gave me a hug. "Thanks, sis."

"You owe me," I whispered.

"I got you," he promised. "Talk to you later."

It took several attempts for him to usher Meri out of my office, but when they were finally gone, I plopped on my chair and sighed. Most of the time, I felt rejuvenated after a meeting with clients, but dread settled in my gut instead. I couldn't be sure if it was because of Rashaad or something else. All I knew was... *Today isn't going to end well.*

CHAPTER 2

"L" Is Gone

KEON

My father always told me to watch out for my brother. When he died, I'd pretty much given up my own life to ensure Rashaad had everything my father would've given him had he survived the illness that took him from us. After Mom died a year later, I went into overdrive to ensure we had a roof over our heads, food on the table, and money in the bank.

Although we weren't technically left to our own devices as minors, my aunt-slash-legal guardian had been more interested in her next man than our homework. That left me to pick up the pieces. Instead of going to college right out of high school, I'd worked twelve-hour shifts at a local manufacturing plant in our hometown of Ypsilanti so that Rashaad could go to college debt-free. I was my brother's keeper. *Still am*. And I hated the thought of him marrying that woman.

Rashaad loved being in relationships. In that aspect, he was more like my mother. He flourished with a committed partner. He gave every woman he dated his all. I wouldn't call him a simp, but he definitely enjoyed the "save a hoe" way of life. Trouble came when the women he doted on didn't deserve his devotion. Like his future wife. Meri Donovan was the type of person who relished in destroying lives. And I'd be damned if I let her ruin my brother's life.

"You're still here?" Rashaad strolled into the building, grabbed a beer, and took a seat at the bar. "I thought you would finally take your ass home to get some sleep."

"Not when we have bills to pay." I'd spent the morning at Smoke and Burn, talking to contractors and ordering supplies for our new Detroit location. Several years ago, my homeboy Ryker approached me with the opportunity of a lifetime. Opening a cigar lounge had been a pipe dream for so long, but we'd made it happen. *Shit*, I'd worked hard for a long time. And now it was finally paying off tenfold.

Rashaad took a swig from his bottle. "Why can't Antonio do that shit?"

Antonio handled the finances and Rashaad was our in-house attorney, while I oversaw the operation. Ryker was the cigar sommelier, so we worked together the most.

Business with friends was a risky venture, but I'd learned a long time ago that aligning with like-minded individuals was money in the bank. Ryker and Antonio were just as much my brothers as Rashaad, and we had an established truth policy long before we launched Smoke and Burn LLC. Which meant, no sugar-coating shit to avoid hurt feelings and keeping it real with each other even if it evolved into a fist fight. Violence was never the answer, but I'd gotten a punch in or two over the years. Beer and bruises went with the territory. Yet, all of them knew I'd give my life for them without question, and I trusted they would do the same for me.

"If your head wasn't so far up Meri's ass, you'd know Tone is out of town visiting with his grandmother."

Rashaad frowned. "I thought that was last week?"

I sighed. "I understand that you have this wedding coming up, but business is important too. And you've been fucking up for a while."

"I know, bruh." Rashaad rubbed his head. "I have to get my shit together."

I shrugged. "That's all I'm sayin'." I leaned against the bar. "What happened today?"

He eyed me skeptically. "Why?"

"I talked to Taylar," I admitted.

"She called you?"

"Nah. I texted about the bill and she told me you and Meri were arguing."

Rashaad grumbled a curse. "Tay is too nosey for her own good. She's the reason why we even got in an argument in the first place. Always talking too much."

Curious, I raised a brow. "What did she say?"

He waved a dismissive hand. "Of course, she didn't tell you how she busted me out about Meri's mother showing up at the house unannounced and shit."

I barked out a laugh. "She's funny."

Shaking his head, Rashaad fumed. "I swear, those two women in a confined space is torture."

I imagined Taylar's patented you're-full-of-shit look and smirked. I loved that she didn't hesitate to tell us when we were fucking up. Like the sister from that old show, *What's Happening?* Damn, she was real as fuck in every way. She probably had on one of those flowy blouses and a curve-hugging skirt that... I cleared my throat. *What the hell is wrong with me?* Taylar's body was none of my business. Period.

"Bruh?" Rashaad called.

I blinked my thoughts away from Taylar's anything. "Huh?"

"I need you to talk to her."

Frowning, I asked, "Why? Ask Ryker to talk to his own sister."

"Since when do we need to go through Ryker to talk to his family?"

He was right. Before they were Congressman and Mrs. Cross, they were Pops and Ma, our neighbors. I remembered Fourth of Julys watching fireworks and block parties, ping pong tournaments and caravans to Metro Park for picnics. Ma had been steadfast in her support of our mother after Dad died and had even petitioned the court to become our legal guardian before Aunt Lenise agreed to take us in. It wasn't weird for me to call Pops for advice about investments. And Ma had helped Rashaad pick out the engagement ring.

"I don't know," I said lamely. "I just don't think I should be the one talking to Taylar about her business."

Or anything else for that matter. After years of strict boundaries between us, something had changed when I picked her up from that asshole several years ago. When Ryker had sent the text asking me to swing by and get her, I had no idea that I'd walk in at the scene of a crime. She'd cried the entire way home that day and I'd pretended like it didn't faze me when every sniff, every wipe of tears with her sleeve had torn me up inside. From there, a sequence of events had transformed her from Mean-Ass Lil' Sis to Fine-Ass Woman. Maybe it was the fact that she needed me, that she trusted me? Or it could've been her big, brown eyes? Her scent? She always smelled like crisp air and freedom, warmth and sunshine. It was bad enough that I'd let my mind wander to her body, but I'd already broken every rule with her in my mind. Which was unacceptable.

"Meri said some foul shit to her," Rashaad admitted. "I thought for sure Taylar would smack her."

I wasn't surprised at Meri's behavior. She'd proven herself to be spoiled, entitled, and unafraid to say whatever the hell she wanted to anyone. Damn any consequences because she'd never had to face them. Ever. I only cared about one thing. "Did you defend Taylar?" I asked, because despite my recent inappropriate thoughts about her lips—and her ass—she was still family.

Rashaad scoffed. "Of course, I did."

"Bruh, are you sure you want to do this?" It wasn't the first time I'd asked and wouldn't be the last. "My gut is telling me it's a mistake to marry her."

"I love her," he replied with a shrug. "But…"

When he didn't finish his thought, I said, "But…?"

He seemingly snapped himself out of his thoughts. "Nothing. The wedding is soon, and she'll be Mrs. Webb. I would really like for my brother to be happy for me."

I squeezed his shoulder and pulled him closer. "You know I'm always here for you. No matter what."

"But you can't be happy?"

I hated liars, so I didn't lie. "It doesn't matter."

"It does," he argued. "You've always been in my corner, encouraging me to do big things. This is the biggest decision I've ever made. And you're not rooting for me."

"Because it's a mistake, bruh."

Rashaad closed his eyes. "Tell me why, man! Meri is accomplished, successful. At thirty years old, she's already a director of marketing at her company."

"At her father's company," I retorted.

"So? She works hard."

"At her father's company," I repeated.

"What do I need to do to show you that she's a good person?"

Throwing my hands up in the air, I said, "Nothing, because she's *not* a good person, Shaad. She looks down on everyone that's not in her social circle. That includes me. If Pops hadn't introduced you, she wouldn't have given you the time of day."

"You don't know that."

"Yes, I do."

He snickered. "I'm so sick of you telling me what to do."

I laughed. "That's bullshit. You're getting married. Without my approval, mind you. I'm paying for the shit. So when did I tell you what to do?" Without a word, Rashaad gathered his stuff and headed toward the door. I followed.

He held up a hand. "Back the fuck away from me, Kee."

"I think the better question should be… When will yo' ass ever listen to me when I tell you something?"

"I always listen."

"You quit school and moved to Texas for some woman after I told you she was playin' you. When she broke your little heart, you moved back home only to get involved with another lady who stole your wallet to buy furniture for her real boyfriend. I kept telling you that she wasn't right, but you refused to protect yourself. Let's not talk about Hailey. You proposed to her in law school, and she dumped your ass right before the wedding."

"I was in college then. I'm a grown-ass man now. We run a business together. Why can't you accept that I know what I'm doing?"

"If you know what you're doing, why the fuck do you keep making the same bad decisions over and over again? The pussy can't be that good to make you ignore everything else that's wrong with her. The fact that she even thought it would be okay to insult Taylar should be enough on its own for you to cancel this shit."

"What do you know about relationships anyway, bruh? You've never been in one. You purposely keep people at a distance because you don't want to accept the fact that you're scared as hell to love someone and lose them."

The dig hurt. It was also the truth. While Rashaad was the jump in headfirst type, I preferred to stay out of the water altogether. Although we were close, we were very different in our approaches to life. Maybe it was time for me to let go and let him ruin—*run*—his life. "You're right," I relented. "Do you, little brother. I'll keep my mouth shut and my wallet open. Come the day of your wedding, I'll be standing next to you, rooting for you."

He hugged me. "Thank you."

"Hey?" Taylar poked her head into the bar. "Am I interrupting?"

I shook my head. "Nope."

She eyed me. Then, glanced over at Rashaad. "I'm glad you're here," she said. "I'm finishing plans for the rehearsal dinner. Figured I'd stop by and make sure my measurements are on point."

"Cool." Rashaad pulled out his phone. "Let me take this and I'll come back out and we can talk?"

When he was out of earshot, she asked, "You okay?"

I raised a questioning brow. "Do I look like I'm not okay?"

"You don't have to be a jerk about it," she murmured. "Damn."

I let out a heavy sigh. "I'm sorry."

She dropped her purse on the bar. "Whatever. And don't hang up on me again."

I smiled. "Yeah, I'll make sure I tell you I'm hanging up next time."

I caught her hand before it could connect with my shoulder. Since we were little kids, Taylar was smack happy—when she laughed, when she cried, and when she was angry. And I'd always managed to stop her before her tiny palm could make contact. "You get on my last nerve."

"Imagine trying the same thing over and again and never achieving your goal," I teased.

She giggled. "One day."

"I'll wait…" Her eyes locked on mine, searching for something. In that moment, I wasn't sure what exactly I was waiting for, though. For her to smack the shit out of me? Or for something else entirely different? Which was crazy. *Right*?

"I'm just wasting time," she offered.

"Huh?"

She crossed her arms over her chest. Then, uncrossed them. "I even stopped home to change clothes," she explained, avoiding eye contact.

I wondered where the conversation was going, and... *Why is she nervous*? Taylar was a lot of things. Bossy. Loud. Intelligent. Confident. But I'd never known her to be nervous. Especially not around us. "Ah."

"Deion is taking me to dinner." She twisted the strap of her purse around her fingers. "I'm not looking forward to it."

"You're still with him?" When Taylar had introduced Deion to us, none of us thought it would last. Because the financial analyst was nothing like her typical guy. He was stiff. He hated to go out, so he barely showed up for important events. He spent more time at the office than with her. And they didn't enjoy the same things.

While Taylar was successful in business, she had a less than notable track record when it came to boyfriends. It wasn't uncommon for us to issue not-so-veiled threats to anyone she brought around because she tended to be attracted to assholes. Men who didn't deserve her. As a result, she tended to drop them quick. By all accounts, Deion wasn't a bad guy. He just wasn't the *right* guy for her.

"What do you think?" she grumbled.

"Honestly?

"Of course."

"I'm surprised it lasted this long."

"Me, too." She let out a nervous laugh and bit down on her bottom lip. My ass followed the movement like a hawk.

"Why are you still with him then?" *And why do I even care*? Aside from ensuring she was safe, I didn't normally wade into her relationships.

"I don't know. It's easy."

"Is that enough?" I noticed I was whispering, but for some reason, I was helpless to stop.

Taylar shook her head. "No."

Before I could stop myself, my gaze raked over her. Earlier, I'd imagined a frilly blouse, a hip-hugging skirt, and *fuck-me* stilettos that accentuated her toned legs. But damn it. Even in a hoodie and jeans, rocking her Timberlands, she was still beautiful. Stunning, really. *Radiant*.

She snatched her hand away, which highlighted two things—I'd been holding on to her longer than necessary and I wanted to hold on to more than her hand. Taylar pulled at her shirt and cleared her throat. "I can just... that was awkward, right?"

Awkward *and* right. *Awkward*, because she was supposed to be like my sister. *Right*, because being this close to her felt safe. I hadn't felt like that in a long-ass time. Which was my clue that I needed to cut this *thing* off at its knees. "Don't mention it," I told her. "I better get back to work."

Rashaad chose that moment to re-enter the room. *Thank God*. Yet, as I watched her—*them*—discuss the rehearsal dinner, I wondered if this new state of mind would soon be too much to ignore.

CHAPTER 3

Pressure

TAYLAR

*O*kay, *so I'm a hardheaded bitch.*

Red flags had flown from the beginning of my relationship with Deion, but no... I just ignored everything wrong with us and focused on work. Even earlier, something told me not to come to the restaurant tonight, but no... my punk ass came anyway. *I fucked up.* And now I felt stuck. Actually, I *was* stuck. In the bathroom. At Olive Garden. With no breadsticks. If I stepped foot out of this stall, I wouldn't be able to stop the train wreck that was about to happen.

For the umpteenth time, I should've known better. I should've known it would be bad after the barrage of texts and calls earlier. I should've kept my ass away from the restaurant. Not that I hated Olive Garden. On the contrary, it was my go-to lunch spot. Unlimited salad and bread? *Yum.* But... when I entered the restaurant and noticed Deion had on a full suit? Then, when my parents, my siblings, and all of his family just happened to be there? I knew I was in trouble. Everyone there would soon bear witness to just how much I hated the thought of another day with Deion, let alone an entire lifetime. Because this fool was about to propose.

Taking several deep breaths, I finally mustered up enough courage to exit the stall and ran right into my brother. I yelped, placing a hand over my heart. "You scared the shit out of me, Ryker."

"Good."

I scanned the small space and eyed him skeptically. "You're in the wrong bathroom."

"I almost kicked that damn door down." My big brother let out a deep sigh. "Were you ever going to come out?"

"Eventually." I crept toward the mirror. So slow, Ryker pushed me the rest of the way. I smacked his shoulder. "Boy!" I grumbled a curse while I washed my hands. "Get out."

His eyes softened. "What's wrong, Tay? It's not like you to hide."

I arched a brow. "Have you met me? I'm okay with hiding."

"I don't believe you," he challenged. "You know you can tell me anything."

"This isn't easy," I murmured.

"Dinner isn't easy?"

Tears welled up in my eyes, threatening my eye makeup. Of course, Ryker didn't get it. He was a man. He didn't live in his emotions, he didn't read into anything. I would basically have to tell him everything for him to understand and there was no time for that. My heart clenched in my chest. And not in a good, I'm-so-excited way. More like a damn-I'm-fucked way. "I can't marry him, Ryker."

Without a word, my brother pulled me to him and searched my eyes. "Don't say *yes*, Tay. And if anyone has anything to say about it, I'll carry your ass out of here and dare anyone to say something to me."

Growing up, Ryker was my protector. He always had my back, against the kids in school, against the kids in the neighborhood. Hell, he'd even stepped in front of me and a coach to shield me from running laps for being late to practice. My parents had grounded him that day, but he didn't care.

"You can't do that," I argued.

"Like hell." He met my gaze. "Did that nigga do something to you?"

I shook my head rapidly. "Never. He's a good guy." The door swung open, and I turned away from it, attempting to pull myself together. "I'm coming."

"What's going on?" My other brother, Maddox, asked.

I whirled to face him. "You too? Did someone send you in here?"

Maddox cradled his camera in his hand and shrugged. "I just came to check on you."

I loved my brothers to death. Well, two of them. That other one… yeah, I barely liked Broderick most days. My shoulders fell. "Thanks," I whispered. "I'm fine."

Maddox shot me a sidelong glance signaling that he didn't believe me either. The difference between him and Ryker, though, was Maddox wouldn't ask any questions. He never did. "Whatever you say."

One of the things I'd always appreciated about Maddox was that he didn't expect me to be the perfect baby girl. He only wanted me to be happy, and I wanted the same for him. I'd even had a hand in helping him win the heart of his current fiancée, Sloane. We grew up in different homes because his mother moved down south after her brief relationship with my father, but he'd always been one of my favorite people.

Ryker frowned at Maddox. "You don't actually believe that, do you? You know, she's full of shit!"

Maddox hunched his shoulders. "So? Let her do her." He picked up a tissue and handed it to me. "Take this." He looked around. "It's weird being in the Ladies restroom like this."

"Don't say *yes*," Ryker repeated. "I mean it."

I glanced at Maddox, who was watching me intently. "Is that what *you* think?

"I think if the thought of marrying him makes you want to sit in this public bathroom," Maddox said, "maybe it's time to end things for good."

"It's not that easy." I blew out another breath. "It's not easy!" I shouted before clamping my own hand over my mouth.

Ryker squeezed my shoulders. "Look, don't panic. From what I can tell, you're just going through the motions with him anyway. At Thanksgiving, you didn't even want to sit next to him."

"Or hug him," Maddox added.

"Right." Ryker shook his head. "I know why you're doing this."

I swallowed past a hard lump in my throat. "I care about him," I offered lamely.

"I care about unlimited salad and breadsticks," Ryker countered. "But I can just as easily eat a fuckin' pizza."

I laughed. "You're stupid."

Ryker hugged me. "I'm serious, sis. Don't lock yourself into something for Dad's approval."

I looked up at my brothers. "Easy for you to say. He doesn't care who you date. Does he even ask?"

Maddox dropped his head and scratched the back of his neck, but the small shake of his head confirmed what I'd always known. All along, I knew my father had been disappointed in my life trajectory. Although he'd emphasized the importance of being an independent woman, I couldn't help but wonder if my value to him was solely based on my potential husband. Which was why I suspected he cared so much about how I presented myself in public, why I made the career decisions I had, and who I dated. I'd only taken one psychology class in college, but I was certain the weight of his great expectations had prompted me to do the exact opposite of what he wanted. In every way. Especially when it came to the men I brought home to meet them. I was stubborn like that.

"It doesn't matter," Ryker said. "Fuck marrying that guy because Dad likes him. This is your life. Has Mom weighed in?"

"No." My mother's silence on the matter spoke volumes. While she hadn't offered her approval—*or disapproval*—of my relationship, she seemed to be waiting for me to finally break up with him. I heard it in her disinterest in everything Deion. Every single time I brought him up, she found a way to change the subject. And Mom always had an excuse for not inviting his family to events. At the moment, I wished she was in the bathroom because I really needed her. If I knew my mother, though, she was probably irritated that Deion had chosen a public restaurant for a proposal. No doubt, my father had been inundated with his constituents approaching him from the moment they'd arrived.

Grabbing my hand, Maddox said, "We should probably go get this over with. I give it two more minutes before Deion sends his mother in here demanding answers."

I cracked up. "You're right. It's time to disappoint the room."

Several minutes later, after I convinced my brothers I wasn't going to bolt, I emerged from the restroom with fresh eye makeup and lip gloss. Yet, all the bravado I'd mustered up even a minute earlier seemed to evaporate the closer I got to the private area in the back of the restaurant.

Deion's father beamed. "There she is. I was starting to worry."

I forced a smile. "I'm so sorry." I greeted everyone around the table with hugs and stopped next to Deion. "Hi."

Deion tilted his head. "Are you okay?"

Averting his gaze, I nodded. "Sure." I waited until he pulled my chair out before I sat down. Immediately, I picked up the menu and pretended to be engrossed in the options even though I always ordered the same dish.

Leaning in, Deion asked, "Taylar, what is going on?" For the first time since I'd started dating him, he had an irritated edge to his voice. "You ignore me the entire day and then you come here dressed like you're going to the mall with Kira."

I wish Kira was here. But my bestie had jetted away to spend a couple of weeks with her sister. My stomach roiled as I scanned the faces of the people sitting at the huge round table. Even with Ryker sitting right next to me, I felt alone, like I was stranded on an island by myself. The weight of potential consequences if I didn't do what everyone thought I should do settled in my gut.

"Taylar?" Deion grumbled between clenched teeth. He wouldn't yell because he was too concerned with appearance to ever show public emotion. "Please say something."

Tongue-tied, I guzzled down the glass of water in front of me. From behind me, a soft hand squeezed my shoulder. Turning, I smiled at my mother. I'd been so twisted in my own thoughts I hadn't even noticed that she'd stood from the table. "Hi, Mom," I croaked.

She pinned me with her eyes, tilting her head to study me. "Can you go with me to the restroom? I need help with my zipper."

I nodded and followed her without hesitation. Back inside the bathroom, I rushed toward a stall and immediately vomited into the toilet. Tears burned my eyes and I finally let go and sobbed loudly. Seconds later, my mother was next to me, rubbing my back and dabbing my face with a damp cloth.

"It's okay, baby," she assured. "Everything will be alright."

Wrapping my arms around her waist, I let her console me for a little while. "I'm sorry," I cried. "We're on the floor at Olive Garden."

"Girl, you know I'd crawl through broken glass for you. In my Christian Louboutin ankle boots." She cupped my face in her hands. "And I will walk you out of this restaurant without a word to anyone, even your father, if you don't want to go through with this."

"You know?"

"Of course, I do. He asked your father for your hand a couple of months ago."

"Daddy gave his permission?"

Mom nodded. "He did."

"If I leave, I—"

She placed a finger over my mouth. "Stop. Your father will love you, regardless. Trust me, he'll keep his mouth shut. Or he'll be sleeping in the guest room."

I let out a watery chuckle. "I can't do it," I confessed. "I don't love him." It was the first time I'd said it out loud to anyone.

"I know." She flashed a sad smile. "But just so *you* know... Never do this again. Never sacrifice your happiness for anyone."

"But—"

She squeezed my chin. "Taylar, I don't care who it is." I opened my mouth to speak, but she rushed on, "Even your father." I dropped my head. "If you don't love Deion, it's okay. You're allowed to feel how you feel."

"I don't want to hurt him."

"You'll hurt him more if you marry him knowing you don't love him the way he deserves to be loved." She stood and pulled me to my feet. "Now, let's get you presentable." Mom opened her purse and pulled out another cloth along with a brand-new toothbrush and toothpaste. "Take this." Picking up my purse, she rummaged around. "I told you to clean out your purse the last time we were together." She looked down in there. "How can you find anything?"

"I know where everything is," I argued.

"Oh, there it is." She handed me my makeup bag. "I have to get you together."

And that she did. Soon, we were making our way back to the group. She gave me a reassuring nod before joining my father on the other side of the table. My father leaned in and mumbled something to Mom, and she responded with a forceful whisper against his ear. I waited for Dad to look at me, but instead he just sipped his drink.

Swallowing, I turned to Deion. "Can we talk?"

Deion wiped his mouth. "I have something I need to…" He didn't finish his sentence once he met my eyes. His shoulders fell. "Sure."

"Is everything okay, dear?" Deion's mother asked.

"They're fine, Gladys," my mother said. "Let them talk."

Ryker squeezed my hand. "I'm here and ready when you are."

I smiled. "I'm good."

Deion walked away from the table without another word. I found him outside on a bench in front of the restaurant and sat next to him.

"You don't want to marry me," he murmured.

I stared up at the night sky, focusing on the glimpse of the moon between the clouds. "No."

"Why?"

"I'm not…" *Ready* died on my lips because it was a lie. Because if I loved him, I would've happily agreed to be his wife. "I care for you. I believe you're a good man. One of the best. Just not the man for me."

Deion looked at me, tears standing in his eyes. "When did you know?"

"Almost immediately."

He dropped his head. "Then, why did you stay with me for so long?"

"I wanted it to work. You were my friend and I thought it was me. Then, we settled into this life, this routine of being with each other. Your parents, my dad… They expected us to be together and I got lost in trying to be the woman you—and they—thought I was."

"Is there someone else?"

"No, Deion." I gripped his hand in mine. "I would never cheat on you. It's not you. It's not even me. It's just us. If I marry you, I won't be happy. And you won't be either."

"You don't know that."

I sucked in a shaky breath. "I do."

"I love you."

"I love you too. But not like I should love the man I'm gonna marry. If I was a bride asking for my services, all kinds of red flags would fly in that Get to Know Us Meeting. I've seen it time and again. People marry for so many wrong reasons and sometimes it works for them. Most of the time, it doesn't."

Deion wiped his face. "You're right. I knew your heart wasn't in it. I've known for a long time. And if I'm being honest, I probably got carried away with how good we look on paper together."

"Exactly. We're awesome on paper."

"A mess in reality." He chuckled. "Can you believe I was going to propose at Olive Garden?"

I laughed. "It's the breadsticks. They get you every time."

"You love it. It's low-key, like you like." Deion really did know me well. Which was why this was so damn sad. But necessary. "I just wanted to give you what you love."

"Under different circumstances, without so many people around," —and a different guy —"It would've been perfect."

He stood and held out his hand. I slipped mine into his and let him pull me up. "Why don't you go ahead and leave.

I'll handle my family because I'm sure your family figured out what's going on."

I bit down on my bottom lip. "You know Ryker is nosey as fuck."

Deion hugged me then, and I clung to him, knowing that I'd miss the warmth and safety he'd always provided. I knew I was doing the right thing, but *damn*... this shit hurt. I felt his lips on my brow before he whispered, "I'll move out. Just give me some time to find something else."

I couldn't bring myself to look at him. "Okay. I'll stay at a hotel or with Ryker until I hear from you."

He finally pulled back and rubbed my cheek. "Take care, Taylar."

"I will. You too."

A few seconds later, he disappeared into the restaurant, and I got in my car and left.

CHAPTER 4
After Hours

KEON

By the time I'd left Smoke and Burn, I was tired as hell and pissed at everything. I still had shit to do, though. After a quick dinner, I stopped by my childhood home. The house was quiet, as expected. Basically untouched except for the few minor renovations we'd done over the years. The furniture still looked new, the kitchen walls were still yellow, and the white laminate floor needed to be replaced. My aunt had actually done the right thing and cleaned up before she married her fourth husband and moved out a couple of months ago. Which was no small feat considering she never lifted a finger to do anything but point at us and tell us to grab the remote.

I glanced up the stairs near the front door, then grudgingly made my way up. Seventeen years later, and I could still hear my mother's voice in the hallway calling to my father. I could also hear her loud cries once she realized he wouldn't come home again.

Before my parents died, my world consisted of video games, girls, and school. I never worried about money, time, or tomorrow. In one moment, everything changed. I remembered the day Dad died clearly because I was with him. My father had devoted his entire work life to the same automotive plant I ended up at after high school graduation. He'd worked every shift, from days to midnights. Most evenings, we ate without him. On the weekends, we attended family functions without him. So we'd always made the most of the moments we could spend with him.

That particular fall morning had started with yard work and ended with breakfast at his favorite restaurant, Luca's Coney Island. He'd ordered his usual pancakes, eggs, and bacon. We'd discussed school activities, my first part-time job, and my college plans. After we ate, we went back to the house and finished raking the lawn. I'd just returned from the garage when I saw him on the ground. Despite my quick thinking, the 9-1-1 call, the CPR I'd performed, the prayers... he was pronounced dead shortly after the ambulance rushed him to the hospital.

After that, my mother was never the same. She'd basically given up on life—and us. That's when I took over. The rest of the school year had been a blur as I'd shifted from a kid with no responsibilities to having the wellbeing of my entire family on my shoulders. And when my mother had a nervous breakdown before junior prom, things got even worse. She passed away the summer after Dad. The doctors said it was a tumor, but I'd always thought she'd died from a broken heart.

I stared at the wall in the room that was once theirs. For a brief moment, I imagined her smiling at me while my father twirled her around the room to the latest R&B jam. Back then, I believed in possibilities in the ways a man could love a woman and feel loved by a woman, because they'd been the blueprint. My father didn't leave without telling us he loved us. My mother never let us go to bed without a hug and kiss.

Rashaad inherited that spirit and applied the lessons in his life. Me, on the other hand? I'd decided it was easier to keep my feelings to myself.

My phone buzzed, snapping me out of my memories. I glanced at the screen and thought about my next step. I really didn't want to be bothered, but my sense of duty never allowed me to ignore the calls, so I picked up. "What's up, Auntie?"

"Hey, baby."

I heard the lighter in the background and figured she was lighting up her twentieth cigarette of the day.

"Did you get my messages?"

"I saw that you texted me, but you only said, 'Hi'. What's up?"

"I was wondering if you'd mind if I moved back into the house? I don't think it's going to work with Kenneth."

Already? "What did he do?"

"Nothing. That's what he did. Absolutely nothing."

Out of the corner of my eye, I caught a glimmer of light coming from the back of the house. "Don't you want to try counseling first?" I opened the blinds and noticed the bonus room above the garage was lit up. I struggled to recall a conversation or anything that could explain why anyone would be there, but nothing came to mind.

The room had been our hiding place as kids. Not just for me, but for our friends. We called it "The Spot." My father built it because he understood that we might need a space that was our own, somewhere we could go to get away from the world. That didn't change when he died. In fact, we'd used it more. It was our meeting place, our game room, our retreat, our private date zone. I lost my virginity in that room and broke up with one of my girlfriends up there. Even after we moved out, I'd given my friends permission to go there, and only a few of them had keys.

"Keon?" Aunt Lenise called, "Are you listening to me?"

"Sorry. I got distracted. You need to move back?"

"Yeah. I can pay you rent."

Yeah, right. "On time?"

"Yes, nephew."

"Maybe you should find another place to stay. I'm thinking of making some changes. Possibly selling or turning it into an Airbnb or something."

"What? Why?"

"Because it doesn't make sense to keep it and maintain it."

"I'll buy it from you."

"With what money? I just gave you $1,500 last week because you couldn't pay to get your car fixed."

"Wow. You're keeping score?"

I took a look in the bathroom and then jogged down the stairs. "You know I'm not. I've never even asked you to pay me back."

"Why you doing me like this? I took care of you."

I rolled my eyes as I turned out the lights and locked up the house. Debating my truth with her lies was a futile endeavor. "We'll talk about it later in the week."

"Promise?"

"Yeah." I ended the call and took the stairs to the bonus room two at a time. I tried to turn the knob and was surprised it was unlocked. I opened the door and peeked in. When I didn't see anyone, I stepped inside and barely escaped a swinging bat to my head. Someone screamed and I blocked a flashlight from connecting with my eye. "What the…?"

"Keon?"

"Taylar?" I snatched the bat from her hand and set the flashlight on the countertop. "What are you doing here?"

She sighed. "I needed a place to go."

I took a second to assess her, noting her puffy eyes and the tattered pieces of tissue on her face. I also smelled the alcohol on her breath. "What's going on?"

She plopped down on the couch and tucked her legs under her butt. "I didn't want to go to my parents."

"What about home? Don't you have your own place?"

"Deion is there," she slurred. "I can't go there."

My overwhelming instinct to protect her kicked in. "Did he do something to you?"

Taylar shook her head. "Nope." She smacked her palms on her thighs. "I did something to him, though." Her chin trembled. "He was such a gentleman, and I still broke his heart." She choked out a sob. "I'm such a bitch."

I picked up the bottle of D'USSÉ XO. "How much of this did you drink?"

"A lot." She burped. "Sorry."

I walked over to the sink and filled up a glass of water. It wasn't bottled, but it would have to do. I handed it to her. "Drink this."

"It's not filtered."

"Do you have any other suggestions?" I countered. "Nobody lives here."

She raised her hand. "I have bottled water. In my car. I parked on the street."

Closing my eyes, I grumbled a curse. I hadn't even noticed her car when I got there. "Be right back. Where are your keys?"

Shrugging, Taylar said, "I don't know."

I shook her coat and felt the outside of her pockets. Luckily, the keys were in there because I wasn't about to go through her purse. Without a word, I ran to her car, grabbed the case of water she kept in her trunk and carried it up to the bonus room.

"Can I have it in a glass?" she asked, peering at the one on the table. "That one's dusty. Wash it first."

"You're bossy." *And so damn cute.* Even with messy hair and wild eyes.

"Occupational hazard," she muttered.

A few minutes later, I handed her a clean glass of water and a bag of chips I'd found in a cabinet. "You need to eat something."

"I am hungry. And I didn't even get to eat breadsticks and salad." She dissolved into another fit of tears and plopped her head on my shoulder. "I suck."

And I'm in trouble. I blew out a slow breath. My hand hovered above her as I warred with myself about whether to console her with words or touch. In the end, I patted her back lightly. Just barely. "I can order you some food."

She gripped my shirt and wiped her face with the fabric. "I'll probably never eat Olive Garden again. It's too much."

I couldn't help but smile at her antics. Generally, I couldn't stand dramatic people, but Drunk Taylar was hilarious. "I'm sure you'll be able to eat there again."

Wide eyes flew to mine, and she shook her head. "You weren't there. It was bad."

"It couldn't have been that bad."

"Remember when I told you Deion invited me to dinner?"

I nodded. "Yeah?"

"He was going to propose."

Clenching my jaw, I weighed my next words because I could either come off as an overprotective brother or an obsessed, jilted lover. "Really?" I didn't even recognize my own voice. And what the fuck? *Am I jealous*? Of Deion Alexander?

She stared off at a spot behind me. "His family was there. *My* family too. But I couldn't say *yes*. I couldn't do it."

I bowed my head and let out the breath I didn't realize I'd been holding. "Okay." I met her watery gaze again. "You said *no*?"

"After I hid in the bathroom forever. And threw up."

"Do you regret turning him down?"

She frowned. "No."

"So what's the problem?"

"You don't get it." She stood, fell back on the couch, then stood again. "You're not emotional."

I wasn't sure why it bothered me that she thought I didn't have emotions, but it did. "Wow."

"I didn't mean it like that." Taylar mumbled something about two-minute sex and big-ass dicks as she paced the floor. She also bumped into the chair, the pool table, the sofa, and the entertainment center. And she nearly toppled over on the bean bag chair.

Unable to take it anymore, I guided her back to the couch and gingerly prompted her to take a seat. "Drink this," I ordered, pushing the glass of water at her. "I'm not going to listen to you until you finish this."

"You suck too." She gulped the water down and fell back against the cushion. "Do you think I'm wrong?"

"I have no idea what to think?" I admitted.

She smacked my shoulder and she gasped. Then, she clapped. "I finally got you!"

Surprised myself, I muttered, "Don't mention it,"

"I'm definitely going to mention it." She tried to smack me again, but I blocked it this time. "Aw, damn."

Sighing, I poured her another glass of water. "You're going to hate yourself in the morning."

"Slewsnash," she slurred. "Shoeslashes. No, um…"

I cracked up. "Newsflash?"

Lifting her arms in the air, she shouted," Yes! That's the word. Anyway, I already hate myself for hurting his feelings."

I raised a brow. "Did he tell you his feelings were hurt?"

She leaned closer. "He cried," she whispered.

I grimaced. "Oh."

"And I cried."

"You're still crying," I pointed out.

"Right." She reached her hand toward my face.

I dodged the contact. "Taylar." She was relentless, though,

and soon I'd grabbed both of her wrists and held them above her head. "Stop."

"You never let me touch you."

"Why do you want to touch me?"

"I don't."

"Okay, then. Stop." I set her hands down on her lap. "Keep your hands right there."

Wiping her eyes with her sleeve, she wrinkled her nose. "I probably look stupid to you."

My shoulders fell. "Never," I whispered.

"I want to be like you when I grow up."

I laughed again. "You're already grown."

"Seriously, you don't care about anything. You don't have to answer to anyone. You don't take shit from nobody." I flinched when she gripped my bicep. "You have muscles. You're strong. And you work all the time."

I used to think my inability to be bothered, to compartmentalize, was my strength. Yet, hearing her say it... Her description of me was pretty damn sad. "It's not really a good thing. You don't want to be like me."

She searched my eyes. "Do *you* want to be like you?"

I reached out and ran a finger under her eye, caught a tear that escaped. "Today, I don't."

Closing her eyes, she hummed. "You smell good."

Silence enveloped us. Under normal circumstances, this would be the time I'd jump up and offer to drive her home, but I sat my ass right there and let her stare at me. For what seemed like forever.

Then, I felt her lips brush against mine, tasted the hint of chocolate and blackberries on her lips. I froze, torn between pulling her close and pushing her away. But, far too soon, she took the choice away from me and backed away. The corners of her mouth quirked up. "You taste good too," she murmured, before falling back on the sofa.

I blinked.

Once again, I had no idea what to think about the turn of events in the bonus room. When I'd arrived at my parents' house, I hadn't planned on seeing Taylar, let alone kissing her. It wasn't a passionate kiss or even a promise of something more, but it was so sweet, so innocent, so good… I knew I'd remember it forever.

Taylar mumbled something incoherent, before she turned on her side. I covered her with the blanket that I kept on the couch. I stared at her for a moment. She looked peaceful, snoring softly, while my noisy thoughts were focused on her and the softness of her mouth. While she was drunk on the D'USSÉ, I'd felt lost in her. And I hadn't even really kissed her back.

Resting my head against the back of the sofa, I kicked my feet up on the coffee table and closed my eyes. I'd known Taylar since we were kids, but I'd never *seen* her or *felt* her the way I had tonight. I couldn't pinpoint when it all had changed, I just knew everything was different.

CHAPTER 5
All The Things

TAYLAR

I*t's hot as fuck.*

The excruciating headache right behind my eyes prevented me from opening them. I tugged at my collar, realizing I still had my hoodie on. I pulled it off and burrowed into a pillow. *Five. More. Minutes.* However, instead of feeling relief without my bulky sweatshirt, I was still burning up. My foot felt like it was in a pot of boiling water. I adjusted my position and pulled off one of my socks, but my other foot was under something heavy, something hard. I tried maneuvering my way out of... *Is it a blanket?* Whatever it was didn't budge. Grumbling, I kicked it.

And *it* said, "Ouch."

"What the...?" I sat up straight, eyes wide open and head on fire. Immediately, I squeezed my eyes shut again, but I did catch a glimpse of a black arm. *A nice one too.* Then, it all came back to me. *Last night. The disastrous non-proposal. The bonus room. Keon.*

"Oh shit," I mumbled. *The kiss.*

He squeezed my hot foot, which incidentally made my entire body warm. "You kicked me," he said. The low rasp in his voice went straight to my pussy. Which was so inappropriate considering the boyfriend I dumped last night still lived in our shared apartment. It was bad enough that I'd kissed my brother's best friend, but damn. One more drink and I probably would've let him fuck me on the pool table. Or on the kitchenette counter. Or on the bean bag chair. Anywhere, really.

It had been weeks since Deion and I got busy. More like three months, ten days. I kept telling myself that I could live in a passionless relationship because I had work to keep me busy. Yet, the more time we spent together but apart, the more I realized that I loved being apart way more than I liked being together. I still loved sex, though. Just not with Deion.

I'm so horny.

"What?" he asked.

"Oh no," I whispered. "I said that out loud, didn't I?"

Keon snatched his warmth away from me in that moment and I listened as he walked far away from me. "You did."

Three. Two. One. I opened my eyes slowly and stared at the popcorn ceiling. "That wasn't directed to you."

"It doesn't matter," he said. "Are you hungry?"

"Are you going to cook?"

"Hell, nah."

"I guess I should eat something." I sat up and felt my hair. My *crunchy* hair. I imagined my face didn't look any better. Runny mascara, crooked lashes, dry skin. Nightly skin care was integral to flawless skin, and not only did I *not* take my makeup off, I also didn't moisturize.

"Taylar?"

I rubbed my temples. "Yes?"

"Did you want to stay here a little longer?"

I looked at him then. Keon wasn't a small man by any

means. He was more like a tree—tall, brown, and thick in all the right ways. Obviously, he spent a lot of time in the gym because he looked like a sculpted masterpiece. His dark skin, dark eyes, and long, dark locs had always made women swoon. *I'm women.* Yep, that's me. He sported a sour expression most of the time, but his smile… Damn, it was pretty.

"Tay. Lar."

I blinked. "Huh?"

"Are you staying here?"

"Can I? I did almost hit you with a bat."

"And a flashlight."

"You could've been a killer."

"Did you think about, I don't know, locking the door and turning on the alarm?"

"Not until you opened the door."

"Really?"

"I was distraught," I shouted.

"Whatever." He sighed. "You know you can always stay here. Just let me know next time."

It was the way he talked to me. When we were younger, he didn't say much of anything. But he always gave me the soft voice. He never yelled at me like Ryker or argued with me like Rashaad. He didn't trip me and make me fall like Antonio or steal my allowance like Broderick. He was calm, gentle, distant. He reminded me of Maddox in some ways—the smart, silent, but deadly type. Maybe he didn't notice, but lately, his voice had a different tone. Almost like he actually wanted to talk to me, like he enjoyed our back-and-forth banter. Which was a trip because he wasn't a talkative person.

"I should probably go to a hotel," I mused. "I packed a suitcase while Deion was at Olive Garden breaking the bad news to his parents." I nibbled my lip. "They probably hate me."

"I bet you they don't."

"Wouldn't you hate me if I did that to Rashaad?"

"Maybe at first." He inched closer to me but didn't sit down on the couch. Instead, he handed me a bottle of water and then retreated to the wall. At least ten feet away from me. "You did what you thought was best, though. I wouldn't want my brother to be with someone who wasn't sure about him."

"You make it sound so bad."

"It's not."

I opened the bottle and drank it all. "This is all my fault. I should've never agreed to a date with him in the first place."

"Why did you?"

I shrugged. "I don't know."

"There had to be something you liked about him."

It definitely wasn't my undeniable attraction to him. "He was nice. He opened doors for me, checked on me during the day, sent flowers to my office just because. He didn't bring drama to my doorstep. I never had to hide in his bedroom when some deranged woman showed up at his house first thing in the morning. I guess I loved the fact that he was a good guy." I fished around in my purse for my bag of mini disposable toothbrushes. Being a wedding planner often required me to think out of the box and things like this often made my job easier. "I've been with so many bad ones."

"Your choice."

"Do you never not sugarcoat things?" I used the Colgate Wisp to freshen my breath and help with the bad cognac aftertaste. "Gosh, could you at least tell me what I want to hear for once?"

He chuckled. "What do you want me to say?"

Now that he'd basically told me I chose to be treated bad, I wanted to hear more. "How about the truth?"

Keon narrowed his eyes on me. "I think you already know it to be true."

"Basically, I'm a fool?" I tossed back.

"I didn't say that."

"Come on, I know you have an opinion. You choose to keep it to yourself. You even did it with Rashaad and this wedding."

"What's that supposed to mean?"

"Like you don't know. He's going to marry that twit in a couple of weeks and you're going to let him."

"I don't control Shaad, Taylar."

"But you know Meri will suck the life out of him."

"I've already told *my* brother how *I* feel about his fiancée. It's up to him to make the choice to be with her or break it off."

"Like me? I chose to get involved with bad boys."

He snickered. "You were on a mission to find the absolute worst guy for you for so long. We all knew it."

"And none of you stopped me."

"That's not my job. You walk around here acting like you can fix your own life, always talking shit, always pretending to know what the hell you're doing. What do I look like telling you who to fuck around with?"

I met his gaze. "Isn't that what big brothers do?"

He dipped his head, but never broke eye contact. "Do you really think I'm your big brother?"

I blew out a shaky breath. He'd called my bluff because *hell no* I didn't think of him as a brother. Shit, I'd named my Ken doll Keon and my Barbie doll Taylar. I listed him as the father on my fake cabbage patch doll's birth certificate. Whenever I played house with my friends, my husband's name was secretly Keon. I'd scribbled his name in every notebook, wrote elaborate stories about our future life together in my journals, and even prayed he'd ask me to my senior prom so I could give him my virginity. I hadn't thought of him in a strictly innocent way since I was in elementary school. And since I couldn't erase the feel of his lips from my mind, even through my cognac-filled haze, it was doubtful I ever would again. But would I bare my soul to him? No, the fuck I wouldn't.

"If you really believe I'm like a big brother to you," he continued, "why did you kiss me?"

Clearly my plan to act like that kiss didn't happen while simultaneously obsessing about it for the rest of my life hadn't worked. "Momentarily lapse in judgement?" I offered. "How about a liquor-fueled mishap?"

Keon barked out a laugh. "Is that what it was?"

"Can we not mention it?" The hitch in my voice sounded foreign to my own ears. Suddenly, I felt nervous around someone I'd known most of my life. The irony was that it felt both scary and exciting.

His expression softened. "Can we ignore it?"

I averted my gaze. "Um…" I grabbed the base of my neck, as if that would soothe my suddenly dry throat. This conversation had taken a turn. Was it a wrong turn? Or were we headed in the right direction. "Shouldn't we?"

"Maybe. Or maybe we need some distance."

"In other words, I can't crash here?"

He flashed his beautiful smile. "Of course, you can. As long as you want. That's what it's here for."

The Spot, as we all called the bonus room, had been our safe haven back in the day. We'd spent so many hours here, playing games, watching TV, and partying. Even after Mr. and Mrs. Webb died, Keon allowed us to use the space for anything we needed. Which was why I'd come here after the Olive Garden incident. I knew it would be warm, quiet, and safe.

I spotted my hoodie on the floor next to the bean bag chair and got up to grab it. Then, I scanned the floor for my missing sock. Once I found it, I slipped it on. I approached him. "I think I'll go to my parents' house," I announced. "It's probably for the best."

"Sure?" he asked, his voice a low whisper.

"No," I admitted. "I know I'll have to deal with my father and Broderick's trifling ass." My oldest brother still hadn't moved out of the house for real. Every year, he'd spout off his plans to find his own place and sometimes he even signed a lease. Ultimately, though, he'd return home with no money and very little belongings after one of his gambling binges. And my father would have to pay off any debts to avoid a scandal. Wash. Rinse. Repeat.

"I meant what I said. You can stay here. I'll keep my ass at home."

"Because you don't want to be around me?"

Keon's intense gaze darkened, and he stepped closer to me. "No." He brushed his thumb over my bottom lip. "Because I *do*."

Oh. My eyes fluttered closed. "Keon, I—" Was at a loss for words? Wanted him around? Wished he'd stop playin' and kiss the shit out of me? Needed to explore whatever was happening between us? Or all of the above? "I just broke up with Deion?"

He leaned in and rubbed his nose over mine. "Right."

Oh My God, he still smelled good. Like toffee and bourbon, strength and quiet energy. "Yesterday. We just ended our relationship yesterday. I shouldn't want you to kiss me."

Keon rested his forehead against mine. "Right," he repeated.

"But I do," I breathed. "It's so wrong."

"Right."

"Is that the only thing you have to say?"

He nodded. "If I say more, I won't be able to take it back."

"Please," I begged. "Don't leave me hanging. Don't make me feel like I'm imagining that you…"

His gaze dropped to my lips. "What?"

"Want me."

He grabbed a fistful of my hair and pulled me to him, kissing me with so much fire, so much intensity, I couldn't even breathe. I didn't even want to. Because then he might disappear and I would be left wanting him, needing him to ease the ache between my thighs.

Keon was a master at this, though. Every nip, every lick, every swipe of his tongue against mine. And his arms, strong around my waist, holding me so tight I couldn't move if I wanted to. *Damn.*

I tugged on his locs, silently pleading with him to move, to do something. But we stayed like that, standing in the middle of The Spot, lips fused together, bodies pressed against one another.

"Keon," I whispered when he trailed kisses down my neck, over my collarbone.

"Taylar," he murmured against my sensitive skin. My sensitive, *still entirely too covered*, skin. "If I don't stop now, I won't stop."

"You better not stop," I warned. "I might kill you if you do."

He lifted me up and pinned me against the wall. Wrapping my legs around his waist, I tugged my sweatshirt off. He didn't waste any time pulling my bra down and taking one nipple into his mouth, sucking so long and hard, I almost blacked out. *Damn.*

I felt him, hard against my core, and chided myself for not taking my jeans off so I could experience him fully. But before I could do so, the alarm at the house went off.

Keon dropped me like I was a piece of hot coal. "Shit," he hissed, rushing to the window to peek out. "It's Rashaad. I changed the code and forgot to tell him."

"What?" Frantic, I rushed to put on my clothes while he used his phone to turn off the alarm. "Does he check on the house too?"

"No. He probably drove by and saw the cars."

"Do you think he'll ask questions?"

Keon stared at me. "It's Shaad. You know he will." He walked to the door.

I ran over to him, grabbing his arm. "Don't you think we should get our stories straight?"

He smirked. "You mean lie?"

"No, I... did you want him to know what happened here?"

He ran his hand over his face. "Not particularly."

"Because you're ashamed?"

"No, Taylar. I can't confidently explain what happened here because this is kind of weird."

"In a good or bad way?"

He shot me an incredulous stare. "You're not serious, are you?"

"Dead ass."

"Both," he said. I had questions, but he pulled me into another kiss before I could ask him. "Don't ask, because I don't have the answers today. Except for one. I'm not sorry."

I exhaled slowly. "Okay."

"I also don't think this is a good idea."

My stomach roiled. "Oh." I opened my mouth to speak just as Rashaad opened the door and poked his head inside. "Rashaad!" I shouted.

Rashaad stepped into the room and panic threatened to choke me. "Hey," he said. "What y'all doing here?"

"I got drunk," I blurted out. Keon glanced at me out of the corner of his eyes. "And your brother gave me water. Oh, and—"

"I came to check on the house and found her here," Keon interrupted. "She broke up with her guy and needed time alone. I stayed with her."

Rashaad seemed to accept that mechanical, unfeeling explanation and nodded. "Good. I'm glad you were here to help." He approached me. "Ryker told me. Are you okay, Tay?"

"I'm fine," I lied. I was a confused, frantic mess. Definitely *not* fine. "I'll stay with my parents or get a hotel room."

"You can stay at my place," Rashaad offered. "I'll be out of town next week for the bachelor party. You'll have the place to yourself."

Visions of Keon on a party bus with strippers pissed me off, which made me even more irritated. With myself. Because we weren't together. One very hot makeout session was not a relationship. *Do I even want to be tied down anyway?* My emotions were a train wreck of wanderlust and doubt, apprehension and longing. I didn't need to throw myself into another hopeless situation, which was exactly what I'd get if I allowed myself to fall for Keon. He'd made it very clear that he didn't have room for love and commitment a long time ago. *I should believe him and keep it moving.*

I met Keon's waiting gaze, then turned to Rashaad. "I'm not stepping foot in your house. Your future bride might accuse me of trying to steal her man." I forced a laugh. "Seriously, I'm good." I slipped on my coat and picked up my purse. "I better get the hell up out of here. I need to take a shower and get back in the bed. I'll start over tomorrow."

Rashaad squeezed my hand. "We're here if you need us."

"Thanks." Once again, I met Keon's eyes. "And thank *you* for everything."

Keon nodded. "You're welcome."

"Text us and let us know where you land," Rashaad added.

I saluted him. "Will do. Talk to you soon."

With one last glance at Keon, I left. As I walked to my car, I promised myself I wouldn't think about his lips or the fact that I didn't get a chance to see his dick. I'd wallowed over my breakup, and I kissed the man I'd spent many hours daydreaming about. I'd wasted too much time thinking about shit that didn't matter. Now it was time to focus on me, my business, and my life.

CHAPTER 6
Upside Down

KEON

I had no idea what the hell I was doing. For years, I'd prided myself on my ability to focus, to stay the course, to execute a plan. Yet, for the past two weeks, I'd been forced to admit that I was full of shit.

Rashaad's wedding was tomorrow. True to my word, I'd kept my mouth shut and my wallet open. Tuxedos. *Check.* Ring. *Check.* Toast. *Check.* And Smoke and Burn was currently being transformed into the rehearsal dinner venue. Taylar's staff had moved tables, hung drapes, and set up centerpieces. But the wedding planner was nowhere to be found. And she'd been missing in action since I kissed the shit out of her at The Spot.

Granted, I didn't call her either. *But I don't call anybody.* My mother used to tell me stories about how she had to force me to tell her things. Apparently, my lack of communication had started when I was a toddler and had stayed with me into adulthood. It worked for me, though. Women considered me a challenge, so I never had a hard time getting ass. My bosses appreciated that I flew under the radar and didn't get caught up in plant drama. Business colleagues understood that my silence meant I was working. My friends didn't give a fuck what I said or didn't say. They just knew I'd have their backs. Taylar… She'd never pushed me to bare my soul. She talked enough for the both of us and didn't really get offended when I felt the need to leave the situation because she knew not to take it personal. The fact that she hadn't reached out, even to check on the status of my Wedding Duties Tasks, dominated my thoughts.

"Bruh, can you grab this?" Ryker walked into the building with a large plastic bin. "Taylar brought more table linens and other shit."

I grabbed the box and set it on top of the bar. I joined my best friend outside, lowkey hoping to catch a glimpse of Taylar. By the time I made it outside, her car was halfway down the block. Ryker and I worked in silence, answering questions from workers and following a list of instructions Taylar had left.

Ryker grabbed an armload of tablecloths. "I don't think I've ever seen you like this."

Frowning, I turned to him. "What?"

"You've been distracted."

"With work?"

He nodded. "Yeah. And everything else."

"Did I forget something?"

"No. But I've known you since we were kids."

I waved him off. "I'm good."

Ryker raised a brow. "Bruh, your brother is marrying the Wicked Witch of the East. Nothing is good about this."

I cracked up. "You're stupid for that, man."

"Seriously, though. You've taken care of him, poured into him. Gotta hurt seeing him willingly fuck up."

I'd pretty much given up on Rashaad coming to his senses before the ceremony. "It is what it is."

"Have you actually talked to him since that night?"

Aside from Taylar, who'd walked in on the tail end of my argument with Rashaad, Ryker was the only other person who knew anything was wrong between me and my little brother. I'd had too many shots during the bachelor party and spilled my guts about the wedding, about the argument I'd had with Shaad, and about how I felt about everything.

Other than kid tears, Ryker was also the only person who'd seen me cry. I'd been determined to forge through the funeral for Dad, then Mom, without letting a single tear fall. I'd managed to stay strong until months after my mother's funeral. Ryker had picked me up to go fishing on Lake Erie. The first tear fell right after I caught a walleye. And they didn't stop until we left. Ryker hadn't said a word, which I appreciated. He never mentioned it again, but there was a silent understanding that he would be there if I ever needed him.

"I haven't," I answered finally. "Not about that anyway. I told him I was done. If he's determined to fuck up his life, I can't stop him."

"True." Ryker spread a cloth over the table. "You ready for everything?"

"Yep." I dropped a pile of napkins on the bar. "I'm halfway expecting Taylar to yell at me for forgetting something, but I think I got it under control."

"She's been on one the last few weeks."

I paused. "She okay?"

Ryker shrugged. "She's not really talking about it. You saw her that night. Despite knowing it was the best decision, she still felt guilty."

My mind flashed back to that night, her drunken sobs, her sad eyes. Then my thoughts turned to how beautiful she was despite how broken she felt. "Is she still at your parents?"

"Nah, she went back home. Deion moved out quickly. Probably because my mother called in a favor to one of her realtor friends."

Ma had never failed to get the job done. "I'm glad she's supporting Taylar. She was worried about Pops."

"They haven't talked."

"Still?"

He shook his head. "Nah. He's been in D.C. for work. He won't be back until tomorrow morning in time for the wedding."

I heard a scuffle at the door and Taylar burst inside, carrying a big-ass cake. "I need help!" Ryker hurried over to her and took it from her, while I tried to force myself to breathe.

"Damn, Tay," Ryker said. "You should've called me, and I would've come outside to get this." He carried it over to the dessert table in the corner.

Taylar glanced at me before averting her gaze. "I didn't have time for that." She pulled off her gloves and tucked them into her purse, then took off her hat and coat. Dressed for work, Taylar wore black slacks and a cream blouse. The sun shining through the front window cast an ethereal shadow on her brown skin. "Is Duke here yet?" She draped her coat over the back of a chair. "I need to talk to him about one of the last-minute menu additions Meri requested."

Although the Young family grew up in Ann Arbor and we grew up in nearby Ypsilanti, we'd hung in the same circles for years. Our homeboy Lennox recently proposed to Duke's sister, Blake. And Duke's sister, Bliss, worked with Taylar often.

Taylar droned on about the décor. "I think we're in good shape." She looked at me. "Are your wedding tasks complete?"

I didn't like her all-business tone. "Are yours?"

She narrowed her eyes on me. "You got jokes."

"Just a question."

Glaring at me, she bit out, "Worry about getting your brother down that damn aisle. I'll worry about me."

"Damn, Tay." Ryker shoved her gently. "Maybe you should get a drink or something."

Her shoulders fell, and she closed her eyes. "I'm just ready for this to be over."

Ryker walked behind the bar and poured a small shot of cognac. "Here." He slid it over to her. "Drink this. It'll take the edge off."

A blush worked its way up Taylar's neck. "I don't want that." She cleared her throat. "I'm working." She glanced at her watch. "Shit, I have to get to the church."

"Do you need anything?" Ryker asked.

She told him *no*. "Bliss is helping me out today, so I think we're good."

"Bliss? How did that happen?"

"She owed me a favor," Taylar explained.

"Bliss owes me something too," Ryker said.

Rolling her eyes, Taylar scoffed. "She's not going out with you."

"That's not what she said."

"Ew." Taylar shoved Ryker. "Don't date my friend."

"Why?"

"Because she's nice. And you're not right."

"I wouldn't hurt her," Ryker claimed. "I'm a gentleman."

"Just... no." Taylar grabbed her coat. "Stay away from her." Her hat fell on the floor, and I handed it to her. "Thanks," she grumbled. "By the way, I added your plus one to the guest list."

"Thank you," I said.

She pinned me with another glare. "Don't mention it."

That barb was absolutely directed at me. And I finally figured out why Taylar had concentrated her ire on me. She was pissed. *And jealous*. Late last week, I'd sent her a text asking if it was too late to change my RSVP to two instead of one. I'd requested the same menu selection as well. The only thing I hadn't given her was a name, my mother's co-worker, Frances Hunter.

The house phone rang, and Ryker answered the call. I glanced back at him before turning to Taylar. "I'm sure Mrs. Hunter will appreciate the fact that you were able to accommodate her."

"Mrs. Hunter?" She arched a brow. "Please. Just admit you're a dirty dog and we can be done with this conversation."

I stared at her mouth, noted the thin line of her lips, and fought the urge to kiss her. Angry Taylar was sexy as fuck. And this back and forth we had going on made me want to pin her against the bar and show her just how much I liked that she was jealous of my former babysitter. Since that could never happen, I took a step back. "I'd hate to point out the obvious, but I will. I don't have to explain anything to you. You're not my girl."

She let out a humorless chuckle that sounded more like a curse-filled growl. "Whatever. You kissed *me*," she whispered.

"*You* kissed me first."

"That didn't even count. That was a bite-sized kiss, no tongue, no touching, no groaning, and no grinding."

"That's because your ass was bent. And, *shoeslashes*, in case you forgot, you're my best friend's little sister."

She gaped. "You're making fun of me?"

"You actually remember that shit?"

"I remember everything." She stepped closer to me, so close I could smell the hazelnut on her breath, so close that her scent enveloped me. "Your hands, your mouth, your body."

I scanned the room for Ryker. Although he'd disappeared, he could've reappeared at any moment. "Stop."

"Do you really want me to stop?"

I sucked in a deep breath. "It doesn't matter what I want."

"It matters to me."

"It shouldn't." I took another step back. I could feel myself relenting because I wanted her. I wanted to experience her fire. I wanted to bury myself in her warmth. But I might never want to come out, and I couldn't risk my friendship with Ryker—*or her*. "You better go."

Taylar reeled back as if I'd slapped her. Then, she sucked in a breath, yanked her purse off the table, and stomped out of the restaurant, leaving me alone. *Probably forever*.

CHAPTER 7
Slow Hand

TAYLAR

The wedding rehearsal was the time to put all my planning into action. The practice run was integral to the success of the big day. It was also an opportunity to show potential brides and grooms how much smoother their own wedding would be if they hired me, which is why I was always professional, always organized, always on time, and always finished in one hour. Today was no exception. After formal introductions, I'd wrangled uninterested groomsmen and chatty bridesmaids into formation, assured the bride's parents that I'd listened to their concerns, and promised the groom that I would honor his late parents in a beautiful way. I'd also kept Meri's maid of honor from hanging all over Keon and one of her bridesmaids from staring at his ass the entire time. *Thirsty bitches.*

As for me, I'd given him a wide berth. Even though he looked good in his jeans and fresh twists, I stayed my ass far away from him. The only time I interacted with him was to shift him to the left so there was equal distance between him, Ryker, and Antonio. Not that he'd even tried to talk to me. On the contrary, he pretty much ignored me. Except for when he'd nearly strung Antonio up for mentioning that I seemed uptight.

I could also admit I'd bulldozed my way into that bar with an attitude and made a complete ass of myself because he'd dared to want to invite someone to the wedding. My little "I Am Woman, Hear Me Cry" theme song had switched to the "Fuck Dem Other Hoes" track, and I'd gotten carried away. Then, I had the nerve to act like sweet Mrs. Frances was a codename for his next short-term piece of ass. Yet, instead of apologizing, I'd doubled down on my bitch-fest—until I told him I missed his freakin' hands on my body. *Yikes.*

"You're not my girl."

That shit stung. And my behavior sucked, teetering between humiliation and desperation on my part. And still... I couldn't stop thinking about it, about him. Even now, at the rehearsal dinner. It was one thing for him to want to respect his friendship with Ryker, but quite another to resign himself to being alone. Strangely, I didn't hold it against him, though. I knew he'd experienced so much tragedy in his life. Again, I didn't have to be a therapist to recognize his need to protect himself and others around him. After all, he'd already lost so much.

Bliss walked over to me and whispered. "Okay, who is he?"

I frowned, surveying the room. "What?"

"You've been extremely professional, but you're also distracted by somebody at this rehearsal dinner."

Bliss was a matchmaker by trade. We'd teamed a while ago to create the Mistletoe Match event and had continued to work as colleagues. She referred her newly-coupled clients to me, and I'd referred my single wedding-party members to her. It was a win-win. Not to mention, her seven siblings were like dominoes, getting married one after another. Her brother Dexter's wedding was my next big event.

"Did you tell Blake to fill out my forms yet?" The change of subject was a protection mechanism.

"Girl, I gave up on that and completed those forms myself. Sent the email this morning."

Recently, she'd begged me to take over her twin sister's wedding. Blake was the antithesis of a bridezilla because she just didn't really give a fuck about anything wedding related. She just wanted to get married. I stared at the couple in question on the other side of the room. Lennox grew up with us and was an usher at the wedding. It felt good to see him happy.

"And you're not slick, I know what you're doing," she chirped. "But I'll let it slide for today. Especially since I know this event hits close to home for you."

Bliss was good as hell at her job. Matchmaking was her profession, but she was also a licensed therapist. Her observation skills were top notch, which was why her business was successful. The last thing I needed was for her to pay attention to Keon and start meddling like she did when she'd purposely made sure Maddox was everywhere Sloane was a couple of Christmases ago. Of course, it worked because my brother would be married before this summer.

"I think we're okay here," I told her. "Why don't you join your family for dinner?"

"Nope. I'm here to pay a debt."

I smiled. "I promise I'll come get you if I need you."

Dinner was served promptly at seven. Rashaad was a beef and potatoes person, so I wanted to incorporate his favorites into the menu. After a first course, guests enjoyed their choice of short ribs served with whipped scallion potatoes and sautéed kale or ribeye with Boursin mashed potatoes and roasted asparagus. For people who didn't like beef, the chef prepared roasted chicken with mushroom and truffle risotto.

Meri sported her usual sour expression, but the toothy grin on Rashaad's face made it all worth it.

"What do you think?"

I jumped, surprised that Duke had made his way out of the kitchen without me noticing. "Oh," I breathed, "you scared me."

"Groom looks happy, but the bride…" He grimaced dramatically. "She's a trip."

I giggled. "Tell me about it."

"I give it two months."

My mouth fell open. "Really? I thought maybe a year at least."

He shook his head. "Nah. Two months and she'll be pregnant. Which will trap him because he wouldn't want to leave his kid."

The thought of that scenario playing out made me sad. "I thought she didn't want kids right away."

"I overheard her maid of honor and a bridesmaid talking by the restrooms," he explained. "Apparently, someone in the bridal party is pregnant."

"Right. The matron of honor, the bride's sister. Her baby bump caused quite the temper tantrum," I explained.

He shook his head. "Not her. It's one of the bridesmaids. They're keeping it from Meri."

I closed my eyes. I knew what Duke was getting at. Meri would never let one of her so-called friends snag the spotlight from her. She would change her tune in a heartbeat once she found out. "Damn," I said. "Any chance you could seduce the bride and then dump her the next day?"

He laughed, flashing his deep dimples.

"I mean, I'd tell Ryker to do it, but…" I shrugged. "Too close."

"I've done some crazy shit, but I haven't wrecked a home in years. That time of my life is over."

Cracking up, I shoved him. "Stop playin'."

"I'm not playing," he told me. "But, nah, I'm good. And Rashaad's cool."

Duke was fine as hell. Always had been. I wouldn't doubt he'd already scoped out his Tonight Bae. Hopefully, it wasn't one of Meri's friends. "Sure?" I waggled my eyebrows. "She might be a freak."

He bumped my shoulder. "You're silly."

"I'm desperate." I pressed my palms together as if I was praying. "Please, use your charm to save my friend."

He grabbed my hands. "No."

I folded my arms and pouted. "I tried it."

"You did. I'll tell you what, though." He leaned in closer and whispered. "That short bridesmaid might give me some dirt if I take her back to my hotel room."

I smirked. "And you better text me if she does."

He gave me a high five. "I got you." Then, he ventured off to make his rounds.

Satisfied that everyone was enjoying themselves and had everything they needed, I decided to take a little break to eat. Duke had prepared me a plate before he set the food out, so I made my way to the kitchen and warmed up my dinner. I also poured a glass of wine. Instead of returning to the main room, though, I went upstairs to the office to enjoy my meal in private.

I'd just tasted my short ribs when I heard the office door open behind me. Craning my head to see who it was, I was surprised to see Keon standing in the doorway, arms folded across his chest. Without a word, I turned my attention back to my plate. The click of the lock behind me made me pause, fork midair. Still, I stayed quiet and took another bite.

I felt him behind me, looming over me. I fought the urge to turn to him, to acknowledge his presence, but dammit... *I'm sick of him.*

"Can I talk to you?" he asked.

"Can I stop you?" I tasted the potatoes and hummed. "Delicious," I murmured.

"Taylar…"

I sampled the kale and groaned. "This shit is so good."

"What the hell are you doing?" he asked.

Shrugging, I sipped my wine. "Eating?"

"With Duke," he grumbled.

I frowned, whirling around to face him. "What?"

He leaned down, arms on both sides of me, caging me in. My skin tingled and my heart raced as his eyes traveled from my eyes to my lips, to my breasts. He took my wine glass from me. "You're doing this on purpose."

My mouth fell open. "Doing what?"

"Trying to make me jealous."

I swallowed. Hard. "Are you?"

He sucked my bottom lip into his mouth and grazed his teeth over it as he pulled away again. *Oh shit.* "You're mad at me."

Shaking my head, I struggled to find the words I needed to say. "I'm not," I whispered. "You just get on my damn nerves."

He dropped his head on my shoulder. "I can't do this."

I let out a slow breath. "But you want to?"

His eyes flashed to mine again and I gripped the chair underneath me. There was so much there, so much emotion swimming in his brown eyes. He was an oxymoron, gentle turbulence in dim light. And I was transfixed, unable to turn away from him. "I don't know what this is, Taylar."

"Tell me," With a shaky hand, I brushed my palm over his cheek, loving that he leaned into my touch. "You want to?"

"You're so damn annoying."

I wasn't expecting that. "In a good or bad way?"

"Both," he replied. The conversation reminded me of the one we had at The Spot. "I don't know why."

"Me neither," I confessed. "I can't stop thinking about it."

He pressed his lips against mine, before he backed away. "Why would you even want to be with me? I don't commit. I hold my emotions in. I keep myself at a distance. On purpose. What part of that makes you think that I can give you what you need?"

"Maybe I don't want what you can't give me, Keon?" I stood up and approached him. I smoothed my hand over his chest, held my palm against his heart. "Maybe I just want you? Flaws and all."

"Why? How? You just got out of a relationship."

"I checked out of that relationship last year," I admitted. "It just took a while for me to do it officially."

"Ryker is my best friend. You don't want him with your friends. Why do you think he would be okay with this?"

I knew he'd find a way to use my own words against me. And I was already prepared. "I only said that because I think Ryker should be with someone else."

He frowned. "Who?"

"I'm not telling." While my best friend, Kira, was firmly #TeamBroderick, I knew Ryker would be a better fit. I also knew that Ryker really wanted *Kira*, not Bliss. "But I would never stop him from following his heart, if Bliss is who he wants."

"It's not going to work, Taylar. I don't want to hurt you."

"Then, don't." I stepped up on the tips of my toes and kissed him.

He grabbed my face and pulled me to him. "I don't see how this ends well," he murmured against my lips.

"How about we just take it as it comes?" I suggested.

He crushed his mouth to mine, kissing me thoroughly and branding me with his lips. And I never wanted him to stop. I was addicted to him, to the way he held me, to the way his scent wrapped around me, to the way his voice held me in a trance. I yearned for him, ached for him in a way that didn't even seem possible—until I felt it. Suddenly, my clothes felt like dead weight. I tugged at my blouse, fumbled with my pants. I needed everything off. I needed his skin against mine. Now.

As if he read my mind, Keon unbuttoned my shirt, pushed my pants down, and pinned me against the door. Before I could take his pants off, he dropped to his knees, ripped my panties off and buried his face in my pussy. I felt a release building inside me, threatening to rip me open with its intensity. My legs shook as he sucked my clit into his mouth. My orgasm buzzed through me, stealing my breath as the force of it echoed through my body.

I'm going to fall. But before I hit the ground, he lifted me in his arms. Seconds later, he was inside me.

"Shit."

I couldn't be sure if I'd said that, or he did. It didn't matter because he felt too damn good to even care. And when he bit down on my bottom lip, then soothed it with his tongue, I was once again lost in a Keon haze. Groaning, I grabbed his locs and tugged, silently begging him to move.

"Shhh… Quiet, Taylar," he whispered. "We have a bar full of people downstairs and thin walls."

I sunk my teeth into his shoulder when he thrust into me again, enjoying the low hiss that escaped his mouth. With our eyes locked on each other, we found our rhythm. Slow, sweet, quiet love turned frantic as we raced to our orgasm. And when the climax hit, when we both fell over together, I knew I'd always want to feel this way. *With him.*

CHAPTER 8

The Worst

TAYLAR

*O*l' girl been cheating on Rashaad for months.

I reread Duke's text. Then again. Then one more time. Then several more times. Until the next text came through.

Duke: *I told her friend to come clean.*

Duke: *Don't say I never did anything for you.*

I held the phone up so that Kira could see it. My best friend had returned refreshed and ready to be my second assistant. "Oh shit!" she said.

Bliss hurried over to us. "What's wrong?"

I showed her the message and she gasped. "Oh no." She placed her hand over her mouth. "What are you going to do?"

"I don't know." I paced the floor of our makeshift area inside the church. Because, yes, the wedding was starting in a matter of hours. "I don't know."

"You have to tell him," Kira said. "You can't let him marry her."

Bliss grumbled, "I'm gonna kill Duke for meddling."

"It's not his fault," I told Bliss. "I actually asked him to sleep with Meri and then dump her."

Kira's eyes widened. "Are you serious?"

I lowered my gaze as shame rolled over me in waves. "I don't like her," I mumbled.

"Okay." Bliss let out a shaky breath. "Everything is going to be fine. Just tell Keon."

Kira snapped. "Yes! Good idea." She gave Bliss a fist bump. "Keon is his brother. He'll break the news and then the wedding will be cancelled."

"I feel bad." I repeated myself another three times before Kira pinched me.

"Enough," she snapped. "This isn't the first time you've had to give bad news to a bride or groom on their wedding day. And it's not the first time you had to cancel a ceremony." Kira had worked with me from the beginning, before I could pay anyone to help me coordinate weddings. "Remember when that bride found out her mother had slept with the groom?"

Bliss gaped. "Shut up. That happened for real?"

"Yep," I said. "The mother refused to pay the bill after her ass was exposed too."

"Right," Kira agreed. "You had to sue her."

I'd cut my teeth on cheap weddings. As a result, I often worked for less than I deserved for the experience. More than that, I'd done my fill of personal favors to people I knew. When I decided to go full-time, I vowed not to undercut myself. I'd gone to painstaking lengths to attract the type of clientele who wouldn't balk at important things like tipping the vendors. Of course, even rich fathers of the brides were extremely stingy with their money. So, I'd built certain things into binding contracts so I wouldn't be stuck footing the bill.

Many of the hard lessons were learned by bumping my damn head but I'd also invested in a coach-slash-mentor program, joined several event planning groups, connected with industry professionals at conferences, and even shadowed a successful planner in the Detroit area on my off days. In my short time in the business, I'd seen more than my fair share of drama. The only difference was… *I didn't really know those people.*

Rashaad was my friend, my family. While I talked mad shit about Meri, I didn't want to hurt him. I wanted him to cancel the wedding on his own terms, not because she broke his heart.

"Hon?" Kira smoothed a hand over my back. "What do you need?"

"I guess I need to talk to Keon."

Duty called shortly after we got busy last night. Before the repeat, before a necessary discussion about what had transpired, my alarm went off signaling that I needed to wrap things up. Keon left—without saying goodbye yet again—leaving me to get dressed and fix my face so that no one could tell that I'd been freshly fucked. Then, I'd rushed back to the rehearsal dinner to check on my clients and pack up my shit while the fellas dipped early to take Rashaad out for one last night as a single man.

When I didn't move, Kira bumped me. "What are you waiting for?"

After everything that happened between us, I didn't want the first time I saw Keon in the light of day to be about Rashaad. I also wasn't sure where we even stood with each other. I looked at Bliss and Kira, who'd busied themselves with wedding stuff. I wanted to tell them everything, but I needed to sort out my true feelings first. *Or maybe not.*

"We had sex," I confessed.

Kira choked on her water. "What the…?"

"I knew it." Bliss handed Kira a tissue. "When you two disappeared last night?"

"Last night?" Kira glanced at Bliss, then at me. Then, back at Bliss again. "What? What the fuck happened last night?"

"You missed a lot, Kira," I said flatly. "And I don't have time to tell you everything."

Bliss leaned in. "Did he initiate it? Because the way he was watching you and Duke… Girl!"

"Duke?" Kira asked. "You were flirting with Duke?"

"And I saw him follow you when you went upstairs," Bliss continued.

Kira held up her hand. "Wait." She blew out a breath. "Back the fuck up. Just for clarification. Who exactly did you sleep with? Rashaad or Keon?"

I frowned. "Rashaad? Why would I sleep with Rashaad?"

"That's what I wondered," Kira said. "Okay, so you slept with Keon. When did he… Never mind. How did y'all go from barely talking to fucking at the rehearsal dinner?"

"We talk," I argued.

"Keon doesn't talk to anyone," Kira retorted. "He just scowls."

Bliss shrugged. "He talked to me yesterday."

Kira threw her hands up in the air. "I'm done. I've known him for years and can barely get him to answer a damn question."

"It doesn't matter," I told her. "What matters is we had sex. And now I have to tell him that his brother's bride-to-be is a cheater."

"The only thing you can do now is rip the Band-Aid off," Bliss offered.

"And you have to do it now," Kira added. "We're running out of time."

Several minutes later, I knocked on the men's dressing room door. "Is everyone dressed?" I called.

The door swung open, and Keon was standing there

looking good as hell in his tuxedo. I sucked in a deep breath. "Hi."

"Hey," he said, his voice a low, sexy whisper.

Ryker pushed past him. "What's up, sis?" He hugged me. "You look beautiful." He glanced behind me and smiled. "Hey, Bliss." His expression softened. "Welcome home, Kira."

My girls greeted Ryker and Keon. We stood there for a moment—until one of them heffas pushed me forward into the room.

Kira poked her head in. "We'll be right outside."

I frowned. "Where are you going?"

"Wedding stuff." She closed the door, leaving me with the fellas.

Rashaad looked up then. "Hey, Tay. Everything ready? How is Meri?"

I'd checked on the bride countless times today. Each time I entered the bridal suite, I'd been inundated with requests. I typically anticipated most needs for the day, including snacks, but I didn't carry gouda or lunchmeat in my bridal emergency bag. However, I ended up placing an order at Jimmie John's for a tray of sandwiches for the hungover wedding party.

"She's fine," I lied.

"Good." Rashaad grinned. "Kee has the tip money for the limo driver. Should he give it to you?"

I nodded. "Sure." I glanced at Keon. "I need to talk to you."

He frowned. "You good?"

I peeked around his massive shoulders to find Ryker and Maddox watching me intently. Maddox wasn't in the wedding party, but he was the photographer. I wasn't surprised he was in the room with the guys. I looked up at Keon. "Alone," I added under my breath.

The door flew open and Short Bridesmaid stormed in. "I need to talk to Rashaad." She was dressed in regular clothes, though. Her hair was wild, and her makeup was runny. "Now."

I approached her. "This isn't a good time," I muttered through clenched teeth.

"Don't tell me what to do." She pushed past me and made a beeline to Rashaad. "I can't do this anymore. You deserve better."

Oh Lord. "I can't believe this," I whispered.

"What's going on, Taylar?" Keon asked.

Short Bridesmaid burst out in tears. "Meri is a skank."

Rashaad stood up. "Marley, what the hell are you talking about?"

"She's an evil bitch, and she deserves to lose everything." Duke hadn't given me any details, but I had a feeling Marley was about to spill some scandalous tea. "She's been sleeping with my ex-boyfriend for months. She even thought she was pregnant around Christmas."

Rashaad didn't speak for what seemed like an eternity. He didn't even blink. He just listened as Marley told him all about how Meri had planned to get pregnant right away so he wouldn't divorce her. And that the heffa had no intentions of stopping her affair with the dude.

When she finished telling him everything, Rashaad headed toward the door. I jumped in front of him. "Don't make any drastic decisions," I begged. "How about you take a moment to think about how you want to handle this?"

Keon grabbed Rashaad's arm. "Bruh, let's get the hell out of here."

Rashaad jerked away from Keon's grasp and bolted from the room. Everyone followed him straight to the bridal suite where Kira and Bliss were waiting, eyes wide and mouths open.

I blocked the door. "Don't go in there."

"Move," he ordered. "Taylar, I'm not playin' with you. Move."

I met Keon's eyes and he shook his head, signaling not to stop Rashaad. So I let him go. Thankfully, everyone was dressed, but Meri was surrounded by her glam squad. Her hairstylist had a piece of her hair in her hands as her makeup artist blended concealer under her eyes.

"Rashaad," Meri screeched. "Get out. You're not supposed to be in here."

I expected Rashaad to yell, to throw shit, to kick pillows. Well, maybe that's what I would've done in the same situation. What I didn't expect was for him to say, "No need to finish. There will be no wedding today," before he walked out of the room. Keon and the other groomsmen followed.

Chaos erupted around me as Meri screamed, the grandmother of the bride fainted, the maid of honor pretended to cry, and the bride's mother finished her mimosa before tending to her daughter. The bride's father barged into the room barking orders at everyone as we scrambled to make sure there was plenty of tissue and water.

I jumped into action, contacting the vendors while simultaneously giving Bliss and Kira their marching orders. Ryker, Maddox, and Sloane helped direct the guests to the hotel for the reception. An hour later, I personally gathered Meri's belongings, had the kitchen staff pack up food and cake for her and her family, and directed the limousine driver to whisk them to an undisclosed location. The reception venue, with the help of *my* squad, had been transformed from a celebration of love to a standard, but elegant, dinner party for any guests who wanted to enjoy a meal. Given the circumstances, not many showed up, so I arranged for the leftovers to be donated to a local shelter that accepted prepared food.

When Meri's father returned later, Ryker and I used a cart to haul the remaining personal items to his car. If Mr. Donovan hadn't worked with my father for years, I was sure things would've been less amicable. Because of our family connection, instead of requiring him to settle the final bill one week prior to the ceremony, I'd agreed to allow him to pay today. In all the chaos, the last thing on my mind was money. So I was pleasantly surprised when he handed me an envelope with my final payment plus a very large tip, thanked us for everything, and drove away.

At the end of the night, I'd just finished packing up the last of my stuff when my parents approached me. "Hi," I said. "I thought you were heading up to your room." My parents had reserved a room at the five-star hotel like most of the important guests. "Is everything okay?"

Mom smiled. "We're fine. Just checking on you."

I glanced at my father. "Hi, Dad." I hadn't talked to him since the Olive Garden because he'd been out of town for work. He'd recently been elected to the U.S. House of Representatives and had been required to spend more time in Washington D.C.

"You look beautiful, baby girl," he said.

An awkward silence settled between us, which was sad because I missed talking to him. "Dad, I know you're not happy with me and I—"

He held up a hand. "That's not true."

"But—"

Dad kissed my brow. "Sweetie, I watched you tonight. I watched you command the room, make an uncomfortable situation bearable for everyone here, and still show an incredible amount of grace and patience to someone who hurt your friend. You're capable, strong, and I'm proud to call you my daughter. I'm also happy to see that you've discovered your passion. Taylar Made Events will flourish under your leadership, and if there is anything *I* can do to help, let me know."

My mother grinned. "I told you."

"I thought you were disappointed that I didn't want to marry Deion."

"Taylar, I'm more disappointed that you thought you had to marry someone you didn't love because of me. I'm sorry if

I made you feel that way. I want you happy and whole. That's all that matters to me."

I threw my arms around my father and hugged him. "I love you."

He kissed my temple. "Love you, too."

I embraced my mother. "Love you, Ma."

She brushed a tear from my cheek. "You know I love you. Baby, you have done a fabulous job here. I found myself learning from *you* as you handled everything that came your way without breaking a sweat."

My mother was the ultimate multi-tasker. I'd watched her take control of shit all my life and wanted to be just like her. "Really?" I asked.

"Chile, please. I would've probably told some people off. Especially those messy women asking you for the tea." She shook her head. "Tacky heffas," she added under her breath.

"Olivia," my father said. "Be nice."

Mom waved a dismissive hand. "I *am* nice, Ryan."

"In theory," he joked.

My mother giggled and shoved him playfully. "Quiet."

I loved watching my parents with each other. They certainly brought out the softer side in each other and never hesitated to show affection in front of us. I wanted that for myself one day.

"Anyway, do you need any help wrapping things up?" she asked.

I scanned the room. Kira and Bliss were seated on a sofa, chatting. "I think I have everything under control."

"I have no doubt," Dad said. "Dinner tomorrow?"

"Sure," I agreed.

We said our goodbyes and I watched as they disappeared into the elevators. My phone buzzed in my pocket. I pulled it out and read the new message.

Keon: *Found him.*

Underneath his text was a pic of the garage. After Rashaad

had left earlier, he'd dropped off the grid. They couldn't track him because he'd left his phone, his watch, and his wallet with Keon.

Relief washed over me, and I responded: *I'm glad. Have you talked to him?*

Keon: *Imma let him have some time before I go up there. Just keeping an eye out.*

I smiled. It was just like Keon to give Rashaad some space, but at the same time, watch over him from afar. He'd done that for everyone he cared about. Including me. He never said much, but I'd always known I could count on him to be there. No questions asked.

Biting down on my lip, I contemplated my response. All day, even through the turmoil that had ensued, I'd thought of him. What was he doing? Would he pretend last night didn't happen? *Is he okay?* My mother always told me to "look both ways before crossing a street" and my five-year-old self had taken that literally until I realized that it applied to any crossroad. Whether it was a literal street or a major decision. Of course, I'd jumped out in traffic often when it came to relationships, but I didn't want to do that anymore.

This *thing* with Keon? It felt illogical, it felt extremely fast to feel so strongly about him after a few flirtatious moments and a very hot fuck against a hard surface. It also wasn't a stretch either. Because he'd always been the man of my dreams, the Ken to my Barbie, the object of my written and private thoughts. No, I hadn't pined away for him all these years. But the simple act of experiencing how it felt to be on the receiving end of his affection was enough to make me want to reach out and hold on to that feeling.

Resigned to either blowing this shit up or creating something that might transform both of us into better versions of ourselves, I typed out a message. With my finger hovering over the SEND button, I sent up a silent prayer and pressed it.

Taylar: *When things die down, can we talk about what happened between us?*

I waited, checking my phone periodically as I finished my work. Several minutes later, my phone buzzed.

Keon: *Why wait?*

I smiled as I typed: *Just tell me when.*

"What are you smiling at?" Ryker approached me, hands in his pockets.

"You're still here?" I closed the last plastic bin. "I thought you were long gone."

"I have a room here. Decided not to waste the money."

I nodded. "Makes sense."

"Are you going home?"

Up until now, I hadn't even thought about where I was going. The events of the day had pretty much guaranteed I wouldn't see Keon tonight. Unlike everyone else, I hadn't reserved a room at the hotel because it was my policy to put some distance between myself and the bride and groom after the wedding day. Unless I'd been hired to do a brunch or something.

"Yeah," I answered. "I'm ready to get in the bed."

"I'm proud of you, Tay." A whisper of a smile crept across Ryker's mouth. "You impress me every day, but today… You were a rock star."

Tears welled up in my eyes. "It's been a long-ass day, Ryker. Do not make me cry."

"I'm serious, sis. You kicked ass today. I'm sure Rashaad will thank you."

I nibbled on my lip. "If he's not pissed at me."

His expression sobered. "Why would he be mad at you?"

"We argued so much about Meri."

"We all talked to him about that woman. Not just you."

"I took this job kicking and screaming. I wasn't that nice to her."

"You were nice to her today," he countered. "And I know you wanted to smack the shit out of her."

I giggled. "I definitely wanted to snatch that two-shades-too-light weave off her head."

He wrapped his arms around me and pulled me into a tight side-hug. "I'm glad you didn't."

"I just hope he's okay. Keon just told me he's at The Spot."

Ryker pulled back, narrowing his eyes on me. "You talked to Kee?"

Oh hell. Clearing my throat, I said, "Yeah. I-um… He texted me."

"That dude didn't text *me*."

Lying to my brother had never really worked, and since his blessing would be necessary for Keon to even consider something more with me, I chose to just say it. "We talk." I nodded. "Yeah."

Eyeing me skeptically, Ryker asked, "How often do you talk?"

"Not a lot. But…" I sighed. "I like him. Okay?"

He shrugged. "And? You've known him practically your whole life."

"No, I *like* him."

"Oh," he murmured as realization seemed to dawn on him. He stared at me. "Does he like you?"

"I think so?" I closed my eyes and let out a slow breath. "If he does, I want you to stay out of it and trust that I know what I'm doing." Ryker studied me then, for so long I shifted under his pensive gaze. The silence stretched on, so I tapped his shoulder. "Hey."

He seemed to snap out of his thoughts. "I probably should be pissed," he said. "Kee is stubborn, determined to shut out anything that he feels will make him weak. Which would make you collateral damage if he chooses to blow up his life. Then, I'd have to kick his ass."

"Yeah, but I can't make decisions based on fear of the

future because what if I'm passing up the opportunity to love someone—and be loved in return."

"You're in love with him?" my brother asked.

"No." *Not yet.* "Honestly, I can see myself falling in love with him. He's different with me. *We're* different together."

"I knew he was struggling with something," Ryker mused. "He's been distracted. In hindsight, I can see it was you."

"He's going to be so pissed that I told you."

"I'm glad you did. I'll stay out of it, because I think you two might be good for each other."

I hugged him. "Thanks, Ryker."

He mussed my hair. "Don't thank me yet. You know I don't play about my sister. I have no problem wearing his ass out over you."

Laughing, I bumped him with my hip. "Hopefully, it won't come to that. Who knows? Maybe it won't be anything but a conversation."

"Whatever it is, you might want to keep that shit to yourself. It's probably best that this be the last discussion we have about *your* relationship with *my* best friend."

"I promise."

He motioned over to Bliss and Kira, who were now asleep. "Look at them."

I cracked up. "I guess I better get them home."

"I'm happy to drop Bliss off for you." He barked out a laugh when I punched him in his shoulder. "I'm just sayin'."

"Stop saying it."

He lifted his hand in surrender. "Hey, turnabout…"

"Leave her alone," I ordered. "Just like you don't play about me, her brothers and her twin don't play about her."

"Yeah." He rubbed his chin. "Blake's ass will probably fuck me up."

"Exactly," I agreed. "She loves to fight. Then, I'd have to jump in because you won't hit a woman."

"Then, I'd have to fight Lennox."

"Right. It's just not worth destroying friendships."

"Good point. Let's get this stuff loaded so you can get the hell out of here."

I pointed at him. "That part."

We worked in silence finishing up. Once everything was tucked into my rented truck and the ladies were safely snoring inside, I hugged my brother and hopped in.

I didn't even get out of the parking lot before Bliss said, "With his fine self."

Kira chuckled. "Hell yeah."

I smirked. "Alright, nah. Take y'all asses back to sleep."

Bliss hummed. "Just speaking the truth. Ryker makes me want to forget we wouldn't be a good match."

Laughing, I merged onto the freeway. "Nope. Can't keep forgettin'."

Kira broke out in that song by Michael McDonald and we all dissolved in a fit of giggles.

"One thing I won't forget?" Bliss said.

"What?" Kira and I asked simultaneously.

"The way Keon was looking at you when you opened that damn door earlier."

Kira gave Bliss a high five. "Girl! I know."

They made fun of me the rest of the way home, but in the end, it only cemented my resolve. Keon and I would have that conversation. And I hoped it would lead to something more.

CHAPTER 9
Nothing Else

KEON

"What are you doing here?"

Pausing in the doorway, I scanned the room before I stepped inside. Rashaad sat on the floor in front of the couch, a beer in hand and a case on the coffee table in front of him. One thing I'd learned after I lost my parents was the importance of leaving people alone. Because I'd been on the receiving end countless times of well-meaning people poking and prodding, trying to get me to talk when I didn't want to talk, begging me to open up when I just wanted them to shut up.

I held up a bag from one of our favorite burger joints, Roy's Squeeze Inn. "Thought you might be hungry." I set the bag down on the coffee table, along with his personal items. "Figured you might want your shit back."

After Rashaad had canceled the wedding, we went back to the dressing room. But before we could gather our stuff and get him out of there, Rashaad had slipped out and disappeared, taking his keys and leaving his watch, phone, and wallet behind. Clearly, that was his way of telling us to fuck off, so I gave him his space. A couple of hours later, I went to his house only to find it empty. I drove to his office, but he wasn't there either. He wasn't at the bar, so I took the chance that he'd come back here, back home.

My brother stared straight ahead, took a sip of his beer. He made no move to check his phone or grab his wallet. The bag of food sat there untouched. And I took my ass over to the other side of the room, pulled out a chair, and sat down. Since I'd vowed to never force anyone to talk if they weren't ready, I debated with myself about my decision to take a seat instead of simply leaving.

Truth was, Rashaad wasn't like me. He'd never been the silent type. He was a successful litigator because he liked to talk. When we'd launched our business, we sent him in to talk with distributors and contractors. He'd presented in the board meetings, drafted letters, and charmed reluctant investors. Our one-person communications department.

I hated to see him so silent. Even if Marley had essentially saved the day by exposing Meri's ass and breaking his heart in the process.

A few minutes passed and my stomach growled. The smell of greasy beef and seasoned fries made me remember that I hadn't eaten since breakfast myself, and I couldn't figure out why I didn't buy myself a cheeseburger.

"Remember when Mom caught you up here with that girl from the neighborhood?" He chuckled. "Janet?"

I smirked. "Jasmine," I corrected.

"Yeah. I thought Mom was gon' beat you down."

I nodded, recalling her high-pitched scream when she'd walked in with two glasses of lemonade and homemade cookies. "She did bop me in the head, though." The first cookie hit the back of my head, but my white t-shirt caught the brunt of her assault. I had to throw it away because the chocolate chip stains wouldn't come out.

"Right. Punishment by cookies. What did she tell you again?"

"After she threw Jasmine's bra at her and kicked her out, she hugged me. Then, she told me I could be whatever I want to be. Just don't be a man-whore."

Rashaad laughed. "That sounds like her."

"Right. Then, Dad came home and gave me a condom."

"So practical." He dropped his head. "I miss them."

A pang of sorrow gripped me in my chest as hot tears pricked my eyes. "Me too."

"Before I came up here," he continued. "I went in the house. I know it's impossible, but I could still smell her. Almost like she was in the walls. I know you were closer to Dad, but Mom? She was the best."

My throat burned and I knew if I said anything, I'd wouldn't be able to stop the tears from falling. So I just sat there, lost in my thoughts.

Another few minutes passed. "All day, before everything happened, I thought about what they would say. I wondered what advise they'd give me." He sniffed. "Even before Marley barged in, I instinctively knew Mom wouldn't have approved of Meri."

My eyes flashed to him, surprised that he'd come to that conclusion. "Why?" I croaked. And like I thought, the first tear fell.

"Because she always told me I would marry Taylar." Rashaad laughed.

I didn't think it was funny. "Mmm," I grunted. Crazy enough, it wasn't the first time I'd heard that. So many people we knew thought Rashaad and Taylar would end up together. They were the same age, had similar interests, and genuinely liked each other.

"Mom tried to get me to ask Tay to the Snow Dance. I still

remember when I told her *no*, that I really thought of Tay as a sister. She looked so disappointed."

My mind replayed the part of the conversation that hinted at the possibility of Taylar becoming my sister-in-law. It felt wrong. The thought of her with someone else, even my brother, pissed me off. Because I wanted her to be with me. And that simple fact scared the shit out of me.

"I know I shouldn't dwell on things I can't change, but I've been here thinking about all the opportunities I had to cut her loose. I knew she wasn't right," he confessed. "But by the time I realized it, I'd already proposed, the wedding planning was underway, and I felt like I'd made a commitment that I needed to keep. I learned that from them. Mom and Dad… they honored their commitments, at home, at work, at church, with us. I wanted to make them proud."

"If they were here, they would be proud of you. I am." Emotion threatened to choke me, but I forged ahead. "Look at the life you lead. Dad taught us to work hard. You do that. Mom told us to love hard. And you do that." I hunched a shoulder. "That's all they wanted from us."

Rashaad looked at me finally, and I noticed the tears standing in his eyes. "You never talk about them."

It's too hard. "That was a mistake," I admitted. "I should've talked about them more. I thought I had to be strong for you. I thought you needed me to be more like Dad. And now I'm realizing that maybe I might've been able to handle my life better if I'd allowed myself to…" I swallowed past a lump that had formed in my throat. "…love like Mom."

Rashaad shook his head. "That's what you did. You stepped in when I needed you every single time. You've always been there for me. I love you, Kee."

I scratched my nose. "I love you." Clearing my throat, I pointed at that bag. "You gon' eat that."

Rashaad grinned, peeking in the bag. He pulled out the burger. "You take this. I'll eat the fries."

I stood and joined him on the couch. While we ate, he told me his plans for the next few days while he separated himself from Meri.

"Does she have a key to your place?" I asked.

He nodded. "Yeah. I don't doubt she'll show up tomorrow to get her shit. She'll probably beg me to take her back too."

"She's full of it," I grumbled. "If you want, I can be there while she picks up her stuff."

"Nah, I got it." He eyed me skeptically. "Thanks for everything, bruh. I'm glad you actually got out of the car and came up here."

I chuckled. "You saw me?"

"Of course, I saw that big-ass truck outside. Heard it when you pulled in the driveway."

"I wasn't trying to sneak over here."

"I know. Since we're being all mushy and shit… I feel like I have to tell you that I wouldn't be who I am if you weren't who you are."

I dropped my burger and sat back against the cushion, overwhelmed by the moment. I ran a hand over my face. "Whoa."

"It's true."

"Thanks," I murmured. "I didn't know I needed to hear that."

Rashaad smirked. "I also feel like I should tell you that I saw the way you've been looking at Taylar like she wasn't your little sister." He barked out a laugh. "You ain't slick, Kee."

"You caught that, huh? That why you brought up Mom wanting you to marry her? Trying to trip me up."

"I tried." He ate a fry. "As usual, you didn't bite."

Curious, I asked, "Did Mom really say that to you?"

"When I was eleven. When we got to high school, she changed her tune and warned me to keep my hands to myself."

"Shaad…"

"I'm serious. Mom said we'd kill each other if we ended up together."

I fist bumped him. "That's the truth."

"But you and Taylar?" he continued. "She might be that one."

The thought had crossed my mind many times since I'd found myself thinking about her like we were on the verge of some kind of love thing. Logically, I knew it was too soon to think that far ahead. We hadn't even talked yet. *But…*

Rashaad snickered. "It's funny, though."

"What?"

"I was supposed to be fucking my wife and counting down the hours to our trip to the Maldives. And here we are, eating Roy's at The Spot, talking about our parents while you avoid telling me your feelings about Taylar like it's a regular day."

I clasped his shoulder. "You should still go to the Maldives. I paid for that shit."

He raised a brow. "I think I will."

"I don't know when everything changed," I whispered, scratching the back of my neck. "With Taylar." He watched me intently, waited for me to continue. "I can't explain it, and I don't really understand it either. I just know that I like being around her. I think about her more than I probably should. And I wouldn't mind exploring whatever this is." I twirled my beer around. "After Dad died, that grief was unbearable. Then, Mom… She gave up because he died. Somehow, in the back of my mind, I felt like it would've been the same if Dad had survived and she died because he loved her that much. So I made a vow to never put myself in the same situation. That's why this thing with Taylar is so weird. Unexpected. Opening up is not easy for me. You of all people know that. For the first time, though, I want to." I tapped my thumb on the table. "So there's that. Now you can add that I actually shared my feelings about Taylar to you like it's a regular day."

"Well, okay." Rashaad gave me a dap. "Let me give you some advice then. You've taken care of me all my life. You take care of everyone and everything around you. It's time for you to let somebody take care of you."

AN HOUR LATER, I knocked on Taylar's door. When she opened it, she blessed me with her smile. "You're here."

I shoved my hands in my pockets. "I figured we should talk."

She tugged me inside. "Definitely." I checked her place out, while she buzzed around picking up pillows and folding blankets. "I'm sorry. The house is a mess. It usually is on wedding week because I'm barely home."

Stopping at her mantle to study a picture of her family, I brushed my finger over her face. "This is new?"

Taylar walked over to me and peered at the pic. "Yeah. We took it at Christmas. I wanted Sloane to be in the family picture, so I scheduled a session."

I stared down at her. My eyes fell to her lips. "You're so beautiful."

She dropped her head on my shoulder. "Keon," she whispered.

"What?"

When she met my gaze again, she nibbled on her bottom lip. "You have to know I never thought I'd ever hear those words from you."

"I never thought I'd say them."

"Have you thought about why you're saying them now?"

I brushed a strand of hair from her face, smiling when her eyes fluttered closed. "Every damn day."

"What did you come up with? Because I've been analyzing our interactions and I can't figure it out."

I squeezed her hand and led her to the couch. Once seated, I turned to her. "When I picked you up from yo' boy's house that day..."

She frowned. "Hector?"

Nodding, I said, "Yeah, him. Aside from a few random times over the years, it was the first time I saw you as a woman and not Ryker's sister."

Her eyes widened. "That was so long ago."

"I know. But the switch had been flipped and I couldn't go back."

"You acted so uninterested all the time."

"I didn't feel like I *should* be interested," I explained. "And when you started planning the wedding, I tried to stay far away." She licked her lips, and I couldn't fight it anymore. I kissed her, long and hard. I wanted to pull her on my lap, but I broke the kiss and rested my forehead on hers. "I'm sorry."

"Oh shit." Her hand flew to her mouth. "That was hot. But finish."

I leaned and buried my face in her curls. Her hair smelled like honey and vanilla. "So beautiful," I repeated.

A burst of air escaped her mouth. "I never thought I'd say this, but you should probably back up. If we're going to talk." The corners of her mouth quirked up. "But if we're not... I'm good with that too."

I held her hand, traced her fingers with my thumb. "No, we should really talk."

She pouted. "Okay, then, you were saying?"

"It wasn't until the night at The Spot that I realized I couldn't deny that I felt something."

"You felt like we couldn't explore it?"

"Right. Then, I saw you with Duke."

You got mad."

"I was *jealous*," I corrected.

She smiled. "That feels good to hear."

I tucked her hair behind her ear. "I shouldn't have had sex with you at the bar. You deserved so much better than that."

"I don't know about that." She hunched a shoulder. "Wall sex was good."

I trailed my fingers down her cheek, to her shoulder, pushing the thin fabric of her robe aside. "When I saw you at the church, I couldn't stop staring at you. I can't stop wanting you, no matter how much I try."

Taylar climbed on my lap then, pressing her lips against mine. "Stop trying," she whispered, before she kissed me again.

I held on to her as she slowly breathed life into the dead parts of my soul with her mouth, with her touch, with her unspoken promise that everything would be alright. I pushed her robe off and trailed a line of kisses down her chest. She took my suit jacket off and unbuttoned my shirt. Then, I was inside her. If I thought back on everything good in my life, every successful moment, nothing compared to this, to us together. Because nothing had ever felt like this.

I bit down on a nipple, enjoying her sharp intake of air. I wanted to take my time with her, to spend hours exploring her body, her mind, her heart. I knew her, but I wanted to study her, to memorize the lines of her face, the inflections in her voice. All things that took time, years. For now, I just wanted to make her come.

I placed wet kisses up the column of her neck, her chin, and finally her lips. I gripped her hips and she rocked into me, as we settled into a slow rhythm. She felt so good, so right. And I felt like a spider caught in her web, helpless to leave. I didn't want to. I was so caught up in her, I couldn't think straight. When I pressed my thumb against her clit, she gasped for air and came with my name on her full lips. The sight of her, so stunning above me, triggered my own release and I followed her over.

A few minutes later, I carried her into the bedroom and

dropped her on the bed. She cracked up. "You better get on here with me," she commanded.

I climbed into her bed and pulled her against me. We lay there in silence for a moment before she perched herself up on her elbow and stared at me. "What?" I asked.

"I guess this is a good time to tell you I told Ryker about us."

"I know."

Her mouth fell open. "He called you?"

That conversation had been unexpected but not as bad as I thought it would be. "On my way here. He cussed my ass out too. Then, he gave me his blessing."

She beamed. "That's good, right?"

"It is. I told Shaad about you."

Taylar bit down on her lip. "What did he say?"

"Basically, that it was time for me to stop closing myself off. He said it's okay to let someone take care of me for a change."

She searched my eyes. "I want to take care of you."

I brushed my lips over hers. "It probably won't be easy."

"Yeah. You're stubborn as hell. But I'm not scared of you."

"I'm scared of *you*."

"Really?"

"Well, I'm scared of how you make me feel."

"Is that good or bad?"

"Both."

She frowned. "How is it bad?"

"Because I hate losing control, and I feel myself doing that with you."

She placed her finger over my lips, and I sucked it into my mouth. "Good," she whispered. "I feel the same."

"What are we going to do about it?"

She smirked. "How about we don't mention it? The fear." She straddled me, letting the sheet fall from her. "We just be there for each other, and take every day as it comes?"

I sat up, swept my hand up her spine and kissed her. "Sounds like a plan."

We hadn't made promises of forever, no premature declarations of love. Without words, we silently agreed to try, to offer each other a lifeline. We made love through the night, and as I got lost in her again and again, I realized that this was where I always wanted to be.

Epilogue
JUST RIGHT

KEON

Summer, This Year

"Oh my God! What did you do?" Taylar gasped as she walked around The Spot.

I'd asked for a simple setup, a romantic dinner with one or two candles. On the table. Not covering every surface. But I should've known better, leaving this surprise up to her best friend. "Kira," was my one-word reply.

She touched the bouquet of flowers on the table. "These smell so good."

"Sloane."

I'd never done this before, so they'd took pity on me when I mentioned I'd wanted to surprise her when she got back from her conference. But seeing her face, seeing the light in her eyes, made it all worth the countless texts and phone calls and that annoying meetup. Over the last few months, I'd gotten better at opening up to Taylar. We'd spent most evenings together, we'd traveled, we'd explored—the world and each other. Tonight, I was ready to say the words that I'd never said to any other woman.

Taylar gasped again. "Keon, you got Olive Garden." She pulled out a breadstick and bit into it. "And breadsticks."

"*Extra* breadsticks. And salad."

With wide eyes, she asked, "Why?"

I shrugged. "Because."

She inched closer and stopped in front of me. Peering up at me, she kissed me. "I love it."

I love you. It would've been the perfect moment to say it, but I felt the urge to say more. I took her hand and led her to the couch. I sat down and pulled her on my lap. I nipped her earlobe and murmured. "I missed you."

She wrapped her arms around my neck. "You did, huh? Tell me how much."

"A lot."

"Same." I entwined my fingers with hers and brought her palm up to my mouth. "Thanks for my surprise. But when you texted and asked me to meet you here, I figured we were going to finish what we started back in February against that door."

I chuckled. "We can definitely do that." I let out a slow breath. "After we talk."

"What are we talking about? Are you going to ask me to move in with you?"

The topic had never come up, but that didn't mean I hadn't thought about it. "No. Unless you want to."

"I would say *yes*, but you're kinda OCD. Especially with the toilet paper being a certain way—and the towels."

"Seriously? I'm not that bad."

She shrugged. "You are… a lil' bit."

"Whatever. That's not what I wanted to talk to you about."

She nibbled on her lip. "Well, just say it."

In hindsight, I probably should've just told her earlier. Now, it felt too formal. And, of course, there was always the chance she could say "Thank you," not "I love you too."

"Kee?" I shook myself out of my thoughts when she turned my face toward her. "What is it?"

I kissed her brow. Then, her nose. Then, her mouth. "I love you." Her eyes widened. "You're the best part of my day, even when I didn't know it. You've only ever accepted me for who I am, and I want to hold on to that. I look forward to talking to you every day, to arguing with you, to being with you. I just... love you." A tear fell from her eye. I brushed it away and kissed her cheek. "And I thought you should know that."

Her chin trembled. "Okay, then," she whispered. "I didn't expect that."

"I know we said we'd take it as it comes, but I already know that I want every day with you, every night in your arms."

"Oh God." She gripped my shirt in her palm and pulled me into a kiss. "Same." Then, she brushed her lips over my brow, my nose, my mouth. Like I'd done to her. "I love you too. So much." She hugged me. "You're everything I've always wanted for myself. My very own Ken doll."

I laughed, remembering the story she'd told me last month about her Barbie and Ken romance. "You're silly."

"It's true." She pulled back. "Keon, I don't think you realize how I crushed on you back then, how much I crush on you now."

"If it's anything like the way I feel about you, I understand. The question is, what next?"

"I know one thing... let's mention this every single day."

"I can do that. For you."

She smirked. "Say it again."

"I love you."

I stood with her in my arms and carried her over to the wall as she peppered kisses all over my face. "Again," she ordered.

"I love you," I repeated.

"I love you too. Now. Wall sex."

"What about your breadsticks?"

She pointed to the kitchen. "See that over there. That's a microwave. Wall sex. Then, breadsticks."

I nipped her bottom lip, then sucked it into my mouth. "I got you."

"Promise?"

"Always."

"One more time?"

I stared into her eyes, reveling in the love shining back at me and said, "I love you, baby." And I would happily tell her that every day of her life.

About those Youngs...

Did you enjoy Bliss and Duke Young?

The Young Family have appeared in several of my other novels/novellas.

Paityn Young found everlasting love in my novella, HER LITTLE SECRET. The twins, Blake and Bliss made their first appearance in her story.

Blake Young appeared again as Ryleigh's friend in my Once Upon a Baby novella, BEYOND EVER AFTER.

Duke Young burst onto the scene in my Pure Talent novels, THE WAY YOU TEMPT ME and THE WAY YOU HOLD ME. And he stole the show.

Dallas Young made her presence known in my Once Upon a Funeral novella, FINDING COOPER.

Then... The Young in Love Series kicked off with Blake's story, IT'S NOT ME, IT'S YOU. Next, Dallas found her happily every after in IT'S NOT LOVE, IT's BUSINESS. And, Dexter hooked Charley in IT'S NOT THE HOOKUP, IT'S THE CHASE.

Stay tuned because Duke. IS. Coming! Very soon!

Please Note: Several of these stories take place around the same time. Some events may happen in multiple books from a different POV.

www.ellewright.com

I fake laugh every time I think about how ironic it is to be a commitment-phobe relationship therapist who is also the daughter of two world-renowned marriage and family counselors. Seriously, it's comical!

Want to know how I messed up my life? Getting arrested for stealing a priceless artifact for a tearful client.

Want to know what my biggest problem is? Spending my life teaching women how to break relationships when all I want to do is make a relationship—with him.

Want to know what that makes me? The Break-Up Expert who is questioning everything I thought I knew.

Excerpt: It's Not Me, It's You

YOUNG IN LOVE, BOOK ONE

"Well?" A soft smack to my ass followed the question, pulling me from a peaceful slumber.

I couldn't open my eyes, though. I couldn't even stretch like I normally did when I woke from a much-needed nap. If I did either or both of those things, I'd give myself away. Because there was a man behind me, a penis inside me. And I'd actually fallen asleep—during sex. *There's a first for everything.*

Things had seemed promising tonight. Tasty food, sensual music, stimulating conversation. Dr. Donell Pointer had hit all my superficial checkmarks for consent. *Looks*. Sincere brown eyes, pretty white teeth, strong body. *Voice*. He sounded like hot sex on a smooth, dark chocolate stick. *Personality*. The good doctor had charisma. I'd laughed at his jokes and had even enjoyed a debate on why soulmates didn't exist. Of course, he'd landed on the they-do side of the fence, while I'd stayed firmly on the no-the-hell-they-don't side. I wasn't one of those women... I didn't believe in soulmates or that love-at-first-sight bullshit. The only way to fully love someone was if you *knew* them. Fight me. But even though he was a sappy son of a bitch, it was okay. Because he'd earned a check in my most important wet-panties category. *Smile*. Oh. My. God. That thing lit up the room. And the tiny creases around his full lips made my decision easy. Sex. All night, preferably. But at least two times.

Except, I couldn't get through *one* time without a smidge of drool on the pillow, and not because he'd knocked me out with his prowess. Dr. Donnell was definitely fine as hell. Too bad he had no fuck game. No back-breaking. No tongue-talking. No toe-curling orgasm. If brown liquor was the devil, there had to be a worse name for bad, boring, small-ass dick. Hell? Disappointment? Underwhelming? No, tragic? Yep, that's it.

"Blake?" His low voice broke my reverie.

Sighing, I opened my eyes slowly. *Damn*. Such a shame to be so hot, yet so limp. A nod and a forced smile later, I rolled over on my back and tried not to look at his *little* problem. "Where is my...?" I spotted my dress on the floor near the door. Before I could slide off the bed and race toward the bathroom, his hand wrapped around my wrist.

"Baby, where do you think you're going? I'm not done with you."

Oh, boy. I couldn't help the hard roll of my eyes. *Lord, I promise to do better and not be a hoe if you'll just get me out of here without me having to hurt this man's feelings*. He was a friend of a friend of an associate. The last thing I needed was friend-group gossip. "I have to leave. Early meeting." I offered him another smile and a light caress on his cheek.

He pulled me closer and nuzzled his nose against my neck. "How about you stay? We can have breakfast in the morning. Together."

Shit. He just said the magic, dirty word. *Together* was not what's up. "No need. I really have to go." I slipped out of his arms. But that hand of his remained on my wrist.

"I want to see you again. Maybe you'll give me a chance to change your mind about soulmates."

Like hell. "Not likely," I grumbled. "So, about that." I scratched my head, scrambled to find the right words. Somehow, "fuck off" seemed too harsh. "We don't have to do this. If you haven't realized yet, I'm not one of those women who needs the obligatory 'let's get together soon' speech." Shrugging, I continued, "It's probably best if we just not even try."

"Blake, you're a beautiful woman."

Can he just shut the hell up?

"I had a good time with you tonight." He brushed his thumb over my nipple.

I really have to find my panties.

Donnell rubbed his nose over my cheek and placed a chaste kiss there. "I don't want this to end."

Okay, I can live without my panties.

A mix between a groan and a whimper escaped his lips as he cupped my pussy in his palm—his *small* palm.

How the hell didn't I notice this?

"You're so beautiful," he whispered against my ear. "I want you."

Fuck the panties and the bra. I gripped his hand before his finger made contact with my clit. "Okay, stop. I'm done here." I pushed him away, stood, and picked up my dress.

"Blake?"

I rolled my eyes, slipping my dress on quickly. Luckily I'd chosen the comfortable, flowy maxi dress over the sexy, short black dress I'd considered wearing. Turning to him, I met his waiting, pitiful gaze. "Dr. Pointer, thanks for tonight. But I'm not interested in more of this." I motioned toward the bed. "It was…" I stopped short of saying it was nice, because I made it a habit not to lie. "Thanks for dinner and the…conversation."

Bolting from the room, I slammed the door shut and leaned against it to catch my breath. I ran my fingers through my probably fucked-up hair and hurried out of the hotel.

Acknowledgments

God, I thank You!!

To my hubby, Jason, thanks for loving me the way you do. You are my strong, silent hero!

To my family and my "framily", thanks for providing countless story ideas. You just don't know how much you inspire me.

To Sherelle, Angie, and Sheryl... Thanks for your unwavering support. And thanks for always telling me the truth. Even when I don't want to hear it.

A special shout-out to my amazing street team (Hey, Belles!!), the awesome readers , bloggers, and writers that I've met on this journey. Thanks for your support. I appreciate you all so much!

Connect with Elle!

Subscribe to my Newsletter
New Releases, Upcoming projects, and Freebies!

On Facebook,
Join my cocktail lounge for exclusive updates, drink recipes,
and lots of fun!
bit.ly/EllesCocktailLounge

Visit my website: www.ellewright.com

Email me at info@ellewright.com

Thank you for reading Dexter's story! I love to hear from my readers. If you enjoyed *It's Not the Hookup, It's the Chase*, please consider posting a review or sending an email. They really do help. Don't forget to tell your friends!

Also by Elle Wright

CONTEMPORARY ROMANCE

Edge of Scandal Series
The Forbidden Man

His All Night

Her Kind of Man

All He Wants for Christmas

Once Upon a Series
Beyond Forever (Once Upon a Bridesmaid)

Beyond Ever After (Once Upon a Baby)

Finding Cooper (Once Upon a Funeral)

Jacksons of Ann Arbor
It's Always Been You

Wherever You Are

Because Of You

All For You

Wellspring Series
Touched By You

Enticed By You

Pleasured By You

Pure Talent Series
The Way You Tempt Me

The Way You Hold Me

The Way You Love Me

Distinguished Gentlemen Series
The Closing Bid

Carnivale Chronicles
Irresistible Temptation

New Year Bae-Solutions
One More Drink

Young In Love Series
Her Little Secret

It's Not Me, It's You

It's Not Love, It's Business

It's Not the Hookup, It's the Chase

Standalones
Some Kind of Love

HISTORICAL ROMANCE

DECADES: A Journey of African American Romance
Made To Hold You (The 80s)

SUSPENSE/THRILLER

Basement Level 5: Never Scared

About the Author

There was never a time when Elle Wright wasn't about to start a book, wasn't already deep in a book—or had just finished one. She grew up believing in the importance of reading, and became a lover of all things romance when her mother gave her her first romance novel. She lives in Michigan.

Connect with Elle!
www.ellewright.com
info@ellewright.com

facebook.com/ElleWrightAuthor
twitter.com/LWrightAuthor
instagram.com/lwrightauthor
amazon.com/Elle-Wright/e/B00VMEWB78
bookbub.com/profile/elle-wright